TALES F
DEAD END WORLD

VOL. 2

by R. E. Sohl

CURIOUS CORVID PUBLISHING

GW01465237

Tales From A Dead End World by R. E. Sohl

© 2024, R. E. Sohl

All rights reserved.

Published in the United States by Curious Corvid Publishing, LLC, Ohio.

No part of this publication may be reproduced, stored in a retrieval system, stored in a database and / or published in any form or by any means, electronic, mechanical, photocopying, recording or otherwise, without the prior written permission of the publisher, except as permitted by U.S. copyright law.

Cover Art by Mark Alexander McClish
@markmakesart247

ISBN: 978-1-959860-33-4

Printed in the United States of America

Curious Corvid Publishing, LLC

PO Box 204

Geneva, OH 44041

This is a work of fiction. Unless otherwise indicated, all the names, characters, businesses, places, events and incidents in this book are either the product of the author's imagination or used in a fictitious manner. Any resemblance to actual persons, living or dead, or actual events is purely coincidental.

First Edition

Curious Corvid
P U B L I S H I N G

TABLE OF CONTENTS

MY HEART IS HEAVY AND I CAN'T FIGHT ANYMORE

(From the personal journal of Matt Spike, PI)

I swore to myself that I'd never write about this case. Yet I've come to realize that I've already been writing *around* it for years now. Working aspects of it into my stories, but never meeting it head on. I can't avoid it any longer though. I've been through some stuff recently, to put it mildly. Events that have made me finally feel strong enough to confront all of this and put it to rest.

That's why I'm writing this. For myself. It will probably never see publication. It's not intended for any audience beyond myself. I don't want to capitalize on this tragedy, to profit off of it. In many ways, I already have, inadvertently, and that's made me feel rotten enough, believe me! So, I'm writing this to work things out for myself, as a kind of therapy. I'm seeing someone now about my problems with this whole situation, and this is what they suggested. Journaling, they call it. Of course, like I already said, I've already been unofficially journaling about it in a roundabout way, through my novels.

In addition to being a writer, I'm also a private eye, so I spend most of my time sitting in my car, tailing people and doing surveillance on them. It gets pretty dull sometimes. Okay, most of the time. My mind begins to wander. I daydream. I have ideas. Ideas for stories. So, I jot down the best of these ideas when I'm sitting there in my car as a way to keep myself from going crazy with boredom. Sometimes those ideas morph into short stories and those short stories evolve into novels. Mystery novels.

Mystery is in my blood. I've always been drawn to that kind of story ever since I was a kid. My parents used to fight like cats and dogs. It wasn't always a very pleasant environment to grow up in, escape into books. First it was *Encyclopedia Brown,* and then the *Hardy Boys* and *Nancy Drew* called to me from the shelves of my elementary school library with those magnificently luridly painted covers beckoning me into their world. As time went on, I graduated to Sherlock Holmes (I only read the original stories by Conan Doyle, ditto when it comes to 007 and Ian Fleming). By the time I was in High School, I was reading the noir stuff, Mickey Spillane and Dashiell Hammett, along with the aforementioned James Bond novels. I even dabbled in reading some books based on *Doctor Who* episodes, as it wasn't such a big leap. Who is the Doctor, if not a kind of detective in Time and Space?

I was, and still am, a pretty big science fiction geek too. It was almost impossible to grow up in my generation without getting at least a little obsessed with *Star Wars*. *Star Wars* was the common tongue of our playgrounds. We all spoke *Star Wars*; it was the lens through which we saw the world, for better or for worse. In some ways seeing the world through that prism both expanded our universe and narrowed it. It introduced us to a dime store version of Asian spirituality, while also reducing the world into a stark black and white dichotomy of dark sides and light sides. To be fair to Mr. Lucas though, it did at least show that it was possible for some people to straddle both worlds and ultimately transcend them. In my own life experience, I've often found that the world is more correctly seen as a spectrum of varying shades of grays. I don't do moral absolutism–with a few notable exceptions.

Why was I always so drawn to the mystery story? Why did I spend so much of my life seeing myself as the hero of this sort of story? I don't know precisely how to answer that question other than that it was a convenient and interesting way out of the unhappy domestic situation that I found myself trapped in. I could speculate that maybe I was searching for a positive role model in the heroes of these tales. Someone better than my own father, with his short temper and skinflint ways. Unfortunately, the heroes of most of these stories didn't always deliver in that department. Bond is a womanizer. Holmes, for all his brilliance, is a cold, remote dope fiend. The "heroes" of noir novels are full of their all too human foibles, whereas the Doctor isn't human at all. Almost all of them are guilty of being what we would now call "toxic masculinity". Sometimes I was too, although I'm trying to learn how to be better.

I still enjoy those stories. Not *in spite of* their shortcomings when viewed from a modern perspective, but *because* those warts are so revealing of the times in which they were written and the societies that spawned them. My wife Naomi is a history professor and I suppose she's rubbed off on me. Reading a good old book is the closest we can come to jumping into a time machine and seeing what life was like back then. Seeing what was going on in the minds of people who are now long dead, trying to understand what made them tick.

These literary adventures were often my only solace from a disappointing and painful reality. Perhaps in studying these exploits, in patterning my own life after them as I did, I was really trying to solve the greatest mystery of them all– the mystery of the human heart. Was I really trying to uncover what forces drive us to do the sometimes wonderful, oftentimes horrifying things that we do? Maybe if I could crack that case, I'd also understand myself a little better.

That's why I write too. Not just to stave off my own boredom, but to try and make some sense out of an often-senseless world. To impose a bit of order on it. If we can't always have justice in the real world then at least we can find it in our fantasy worlds. Maybe that's ultimately why anyone writes? We all process life through stories. We relate to other people's stories with varying levels of empathy and can't help but see ourselves as the heroes of our own stories–even when ultimately, we fail.

So yes, there have been dribs and drabs of this story that have bled into my mystery fiction, unconsciously. How could something this impactful not creep into my writing? Remember when I said that I don't do moral absolutism? Maybe that's one of the many reasons why this case messed with my head so badly. For once, I was confronted with something, *someone,* who seemed to me to be nothing but the epitome of pure evil. Pure evil is something I didn't want to believe in, but I couldn't deny it when confronted by it. This case challenged me on so many levels. It almost destroyed me. If not in body, then in spirit.

The worst thing is that it's the thing I've become most famous for, aside from a book or two that was more successful than it had any business being. Most people see it as a triumph of my career. It's brought me more business. I profit from it whether I want to or not. But that's all because very few people know the full truth. My life has its share of secrets which I'm obligated to keep. For reasons that will soon become obvious, I can't tell the whole truth to anyone but these pages, my closest friends and family, and the therapist I was provided with.

INVESTIGATION DAY ONE

I t all started innocently enough. I was even excited when
this case first landed at my feet. So few of my cases are very
fulfilling in any sort of meaningful way. It's rare that I feel
like I'm making much of a real impact in the world with my
work. So many of my cases are just trying to provide evidence
that person X is cheating on person Y with person Z or
proving that someone must be faking that on-the-job injury
because they just went skiing this past weekend. You get the
idea. Petty cases for a petty world. They help to pay the bills
and keep me busy, but I derive very little actual satisfaction
from most of them.

So when I first heard about this case, the case of a missing
teenage girl, I leapt at it. I was filled with the hope that I'd be
able to reunite the worried parents with their child. Maybe I
could also rescue this poor kid from the dangerous situation
of trying to survive on her own out on the mean streets? Matt
Spike to the rescue! The hero of my own story. That's how it
was supposed to play out.

So it was that one fine spring day in 2002, I was waiting
for the parents of the missing kid, Mellisa Hollins, to arrive
in my office. We were supposed to go over the details of the
case together. I always had an in-person meeting with

potential new clients before formally agreeing to take on any new case. For all the aforementioned reasons, I had already resolved to take this one on, but I still wanted to meet the family before I made a move. I need to get a feel for my clients first. There's invaluable data that you get from these kinds of meetings, information about the situation, about the kinds of people that are involved that you can't get from the questionnaires I have my clients fill out before we even speak.

I was passing the time playing around with a relic of my childhood, an old bearded 1970's GI Joe action figure I kept on my expansive dark cherry wood desk. I often put him in a series of silly poses when I am bored and need something to do with my hands. Today, I decided to see if I could get him to do a headstand. It was pretty tough to get him to balance for more than a few seconds. It looked like I had finally succeeded when the intercom on my desk suddenly buzzed, making me jump just enough to send old Joe tumbling off the edge of my desk. I leaned over to scoop him back up from the oriental carpet, plopping him back down unceremoniously on his side.

I pressed the button and spoke into the device. "Yes?"

"Greg and Amanda Hollins are here to see you now, Matt," came the disembodied voice of Penny, my assistant.

I won't call her a secretary, as that might oversimplify what she really did in the minds of too many people. She was much more than a secretary. She was responsible for keeping the whole office running smoothly, from tiny details like making sure there was always a fresh cup of coffee nearby to balancing the books and ordering supplies. She handled all the routine plus vital stuff, so my mind was free to concentrate on my cases. Even though most of my cases honestly didn't require me to maintain a laser focus on them. She was also an accomplished, self-taught hacker and a damned good researcher. On top of all of that, she was something of a musical genius (in my opinion at least) who was the brains behind a moderately successful rock band that she fronted along with my partner, Randy. I was lucky to have her, lucky that she was content to work for me. I'd have been lost without her. In many ways, Penny and Randy were far more than co-workers, they were family too.

"Send 'em in." I said, trying to smooth out my wrinkled shirt and straighten the perpetual slouch in my posture. I struggled to at least present something resembling an air of dignity and professionalism.

The door to my office swung open, Penny's delicate, pale hand upon the brass knob. A young-ish looking couple filed past her into the room. They appeared to be somewhere in their thirties, close to the same age I was at the time. The man,

Greg Hollins, was African American, with a dark mahogany skin tone and a bulky, muscular looking build. His wife, Amanda, seemed small next to him. She was of an average build with shoulder length curly light brown hair and bright green eyes that might've sparkled under happier circumstances. But these were far from happy circumstances. They both had a melancholy, subdued demeanor about them. I couldn't blame them. As a father myself, I could only imagine what they must've been going through.

I rose from my overly plush leather chair with a squeak, maneuvering around my bulky desk to greet them with an outstretched hand. They each took my hand in turn. I gestured towards the two padded wooden armchairs sitting in front of my desk.

"Hello, I'm Matt. I'm pleased to meet you both. Thanks for coming in today, please have a seat." I said with practiced ease. Sometimes I felt like a broken record. I made a mental note to vary my routine a little going forwards as I hurried back to my own seat without trying to look like I was rushing to do so. The morose couple mumbled their equivalent greetings before sitting down.

Penny threw me a questioning look from the doorframe where she stood. From our many years together, I knew exactly what she was wordlessly asking: *"Is that everything you need for now?"*

I gave a small nod of my head and a half smile to answer *"yes"*, and with that she gently shut the office door.

"I wanted to start out by saying how sorry I am to hear about the situation with your daughter. I understand that she disappeared four days ago, is that right? Can you tell me about how you first discovered that she was gone?" I already had many of these details in the file that sat on the desk before me, which contained the questionnaire Penny had filled out when she'd spoken to them on the phone yesterday, but it was always good to hear everything straight from the horse's mouth.

Amanda was the first one to take up the story of that dreadful morning.

"I knocked on Melissa's bedroom door like I do every morning to make sure she's getting ready for school. There was no answer, so I opened the door. She wasn't anywhere inside. I noticed that her bedroom window was pushed open, which was pretty strange because she didn't sleep with it open like that. It looked like it was wide enough for someone to slip through. I shut it. I tried not to panic; I kept telling myself that maybe she was already up and was just somewhere else in the house. Maybe I just hadn't run into her yet? I left her bedroom and started calling her name. I asked my youngest, our son Ty, if he'd seen her and he said he hadn't. He was already dressed and was about to walk out the door to go to his bus stop. He's still in elementary school and leaves sooner than my daughters do. I checked a few more rooms and kept calling her name. I was really starting to worry now." She paused, her face lined with anxiety.

I hated making her relive these events, but unfortunately it was necessary. There might be some vital detail that she'd left out of the description of the events that I already had. I also needed to study her demeanor as she told the story. The subtle things that body language gave away sometimes spoke volumes about our true feelings and intentions more than anything that we say out loud. Over the years, I've become fairly well versed in how to make sense out of this secret code.

I was impressed with the genuineness of her responses thus far. She didn't seem to be holding anything back. Her husband reached out a hand and took hers to comfort her. This small gesture didn't seem contrived, and it told me that their relationship was likely a pretty solid one. Tragedies like the one they were living through tended to either bring couples closer together or widen any existing fault lines in the relationship until it splits apart. I was happy to see that they seemed to be leaning on each other during this difficult time.

Amanda picked up her story again. "I was really starting to get worried now. I thought for sure that she'd be in the bathroom, but she wasn't. My oldest daughter, Dawn, heard all the shouting and came out of her room. She didn't have any idea where she was either. Ty had to leave for the bus stop. Dawn helped me search the house again, and we also searched the backyard, but there was still no sign of her. I told Dawn to start getting ready for school and I called my husband."

I looked over at Greg Hollins. "You weren't at home?"

"No, I'm a security guard at a hospital. I work the night shift. I had about another hour left in my shift when I got her call. After I calmed her down, she asked if I'd noticed anything weird before I left for work last night. I told her I hadn't. I asked her to call her friends and see if she'd snuck out during the night to hang out with any of them."

I interrupted him. "Is that something she'd done in the past?"

"No. At least not that any of us knew about. She doesn't even have many close friends. It was more the sort of thing that we did as kids than anything I'd ever caught my own kids doing. I was grasping at straws, trying to cover all the bases, y'know?"

"Makes sense," I agreed. "So what happened next?"

"I told her to call the cops and report her missing if none of her friends knew where she was. Then I told my supervisor what was going on and left work a little early. When I reached the neighborhood where we live I drove around a little on some of the streets close to our house, to see if she was on any of them, but of course she wasn't. By the time I pulled into the driveway, the cops were already at the house."

His mention of the police reminded me of something. "Did you bring a copy of the police report that I asked for?"

Greg glanced at his wife, and she opened her purse, removing a few papers that were folded down the middle. "Yes, here it is." She answered as she leaned forward to pass it to me. I had to stand up to reach it. My desk really is too damned big and pretentious. It looks more like something that belongs in the Oval Office and sometimes I regret picking it out. I was going for a sort of old world masculine chic look at the time, but I'm not so sure it really suits me. I feel like it makes me look like some sort of a captain of industry, ready to pillage the earth and exploit my workers instead of the regular Joe that I am. I worry that my clients find the decor a little off putting too sometimes.

"Thanks." I said as I settled back into my equally preposterous chair with its irritatingly squeaky springs. I quickly scanned the police report. There wasn't much there, and nothing that I didn't already know aside from a few specifics like times and dates. Cops are good with times and dates, or at least approximations of them. It was written in the typically sparse, no-nonsense manner that all police reports are written in. As a writer of fiction, this sort of colorless account is particularly painful to read over. I swear that a cop could describe witnessing a fight between Paul Bunyan and Bigfoot in a way that would put you to sleep. Thankfully, I already had plenty of caffeine coursing through my veins from all the cups of coffee I'd already consumed. Coffee is the fuel that keeps my motor running smoothly. Not finding anything of particular interest in the report, I passed it into the manila file folder I was already compiling on the case.

"Have you heard anything else from them since they filed this report?" I inquired.

"Nothing!" Greg said, the disgust and anger evident in his tone. "They're not taking any of this seriously enough. They're just treating her like she's just another teenage runaway! That's why my friends suggested we hire a private investigator, and here we are."

I nodded sympathetically. I was all too aware of how the police often handled these kinds of matters, especially when the missing kid was a teenager who didn't come from a rich or influential family. They expected that the kid would just show up back home a few days later, spooked by the difficulty of trying to make it out in the big bad world all by themselves. In their defense, that *is* what happened in many cases. And if it didn't work out that way? Well too bad! Even in the most rural of towns they complain that they don't have the resources to devote to doing anything resembling a thorough investigation. God forbid you fail to meet your monthly quota of giving out speeding tickets because your officers were too busy looking for missing children! As with most things in life, the almighty dollar dictates the priorities. There's money in giving out tickets, but no money in reuniting missing children with their families. The world we live in is truly a fucked up one, isn't it?

"What do you think happened? Do you think she ran away?" It was a difficult question to ask, as answering it truthfully might expose some family secrets, but it had to be done.

"I can't imagine why she'd want to run away from home." Amanda answered quickly. "She's always seemed happy enough. Honestly, it's hard to tell sometimes. She's a very quiet kid, she keeps to herself mostly. It's hard to get her to come out of her shell and talk to you." She sounded a little ashamed as she spoke the last few words. Doubtlessly, she was blaming herself, questioning her abilities as a mother for failing to understand what forces might be driving her daughter. It's hard not to do so under such circumstances. I felt sorry for her.

Greg now chimed in. "I think she snuck out of the house for whatever reason. We always keep our windows locked. Her bedroom window could've only been opened from the inside. Her room wasn't any messier than it normally is, so that's another reason why I don't think anyone came in through the window and took her. I don't think she meant to run away. She didn't bring anything with her, she didn't pack a bag. I think she slipped out of the house, maybe she just wanted to take a walk? But while she was out, something... might've happened to her." His voice trailed off at the ugly suggestion that she'd met with foul play. I was grateful for his analytical way of assessing the situation. He'd already answered some of the follow up questions I was planning on asking. I shouldn't have been surprised that he approached the problem this way. He was, after all, a security guard, a trained observer. I guessed that he was also probably ex-military from the way he carried himself.

"I wouldn't jump to the conclusion that something bad has happened to her. I'm hoping we can bring her home safe and sound." I said reassuringly, then realized I'd put my foot in my mouth. I didn't like to make promises on things I couldn't guarantee. I didn't mean to give them false hope, but they seemed so pitiful sitting there before me that I had an overwhelming impulse to say something comforting.

"So that means you'll take the case?" Amanda asked hopefully.

I didn't see the point in maintaining the pretense any longer. "Yes, as a father myself, I'd be happy to take on your case."

For the first time since entering my office, Amanda Hollins allowed herself to smile. It was every bit as radiant as I'd expected it to be, like the sun breaking through rain clouds. Some of the tension that had been hanging in the air instantly evaporated.

"Thank you!" Greg smiled.

"I still have a few more questions for you." I advised them.

"Of course, anything!" She replied.

"Did she have a boyfriend? Any crushes that you know about?"

"If you're asking if she ran off with a boy, you're mistaken." Greg said a little confrontationally. "Melissa is a good girl, she wouldn't do something like that. Besides, she's only 13."

I remembered what I was like at thirteen. I also had a twelve-year-old boy at home to remind me in case my recollections started to get fuzzy. It wasn't a possibility I could so easily rule out, despite what daddy here might like to think his precious little girl is capable of. It would be negligent of me not to look into this angle.

"She considers most of the boys her own age to be terribly immature. She's not interested in any of them." Amanda added.

This immediately set off an alarm bell in my head. If she thought the boys her own age were beneath her (honestly, they probably were, boys can be terrible at that age), then that was the ideal motivation to get mixed up with older boys, or even worse—men. Although I have a hard time calling anyone who would get involved with someone so young a man.

I could see that these two were in denial about this possibility. If something like this was going on, they were obviously in the dark in regards to it. I'd have to question others about it, like somebody closer to Melissa's own age that she would've felt more comfortable confiding in, like one of her friends or siblings.

"Would it be okay if I stopped by your home later on today? I'd like to talk to your other children, if you're alright with me questioning them?"

"That would be fine, maybe you could join us for dinner? We usually eat around 6." Greg answered.

"Thanks for the invitation, I'd like that," I grinned back. "Did you bring that recent photo of Melissa I asked for?"

Before I stopped by their house, I wanted to show it around at the train station in Raritan, the town where they lived. If Melissa had run away, there was a good chance she might've taken a train or a bus out of there, and one of the workers might remember seeing a kid her age traveling alone. If she was traveling alone, that is.

Once again, Amanda opened her purse and produced the picture I'd requested. She slid it across my desk, sparing me the trouble of having to get up to retrieve it this time. I held it up to my eyes for a moment.

Melissa Hollins smiled shyly back at me. She had long dark hair and her mother's eyes. She looked a little younger than 13 to me, but honestly it was hard to tell. When you hit a certain age, everyone who isn't in their mid-twenties starts to look like a baby. The idea of someone so innocent being missing for so many days made me queasy. I knew that after the first 48 hours the chances of finding her became exponentially distant, and we were already well past that unfortunate milestone. It's why I was so eager to get started on this case. I would've started working on it the day before when her parents first contacted my office, but they got in touch with us too late in the workday and neither of them were able to make it into the office to meet with me on such short notice. I added Melissa's picture to her growing file in front of me.

I noticed that Greg's eyes were fixated on something behind me.

"I know this might seem a little out of left field, but what's up with that big sword?" He asked.

He was talking about the *Vermilion Avenger*, a huge sword with a reddish, crystalline blade that I had hanging on the wall.

"Oh that? It's a prop from a student film one of my friends made back in college. I thought it looked cool and asked him if I could keep it."

This was a complete lie. The truth about this sword and why I kept it in my office was too strange to be believed. I hardly believed it myself. They'd think I was some kind of a nut if I tried to explain it to them, but sometimes truth is stranger than fiction. In fact, when it comes to my life, sadly it often is. I'd had my fair share of adventures to rival any of those experienced by my fictional heroes over the years. This sword was a keepsake from my first such adventure. I can tell you that adventures belong in the world of fiction, living them in real life is often a terrifying experience. I had to remind myself of this whenever I complained about being bored. There was a lot to be said for a good, safe, boring day when you weren't constantly worried about yourself or someone you loved getting killed or the fabric of reality itself unwinding around you.

I thanked them for coming in once more and told them I'd see them again later that night.

They left my office to go fill out a few more forms with Penny now that I'd formally accepted their case. As I watched them leave, I was still feeling pretty positive. I was filled with the hope that I could bring Melissa back home. That there was a happy ending waiting for us all.

What a fool I was.

I'd started my investigation at the train station. I knew it was a long shot that she'd taken public transportation since, as far as her parents could tell, she didn't have any money on her with which to buy a ticket. However, that didn't rule out the possibility that she'd hidden some money away or met up with someone else who'd then bought her a ticket.

I spoke to the manager and got his permission to talk to any employees who had been working the night when Melissa went missing. I was lucky that the same workers that had been there that night had already started their shift and were all there. None of them remembered seeing her when I showed them my photo of her.

The guy who ran the station was kind enough to make me a copy of the security video from that night. Because I wasn't a cop, this was something that most places weren't willing to let me do, or just as often the tapes had already been taped over by the time I asked for them. In this case, I was doubly lucky that the tape from that night was still intact, and they were also happy to make a copy of it. I've since come to realize that people are usually a bit more cooperative when a child's safety is at stake than they would normally be. However, since nobody recalled seeing Melissa that night, I wasn't terribly optimistic about my chances of finding her in the taped footage either. The train station was beginning to look like a dead end. In a way, this might have actually been a good thing. While it still left me without any leads, if she had boarded a train or bus from this terminal she could've gotten into the city. Raritan NJ isn't really that far away from NYC, so she could've easily gotten from here to there. If that's where she was, trying to locate her there would be like looking for a needle in a haystack. The fact that nobody recalled seeing her at the station gave me some small measure of hope that maybe she hadn't gone to the city.

Next, I stopped by the offices of some of the taxi companies in the area to see if anyone recalled picking her up. I left them with some photocopies of her picture I'd made before leaving my office, along with my business card as most of the drivers were out on the road. Checking those places was another long shot, but I felt that I needed to do it to cover all the bases.

By the time I was done with all of this, it was getting pretty close to six o'clock. I decided it was time to head over to the Hollins residence. I'd already called Naomi to let her know I was going to be pulling a late night. I checked their address and made my way over there. I got a little lost– it would still be a few more years before I had a GPS in my car. They weren't all that common back in '02 and I'm one of those weirdos that's slow to adopt new technologies. Also, to be honest, I'm a bit of a cheapskate. It's one of the bad things I inherited from my old man, who was the king of the cheapos. At least I'm not cheap when it comes to other people. I take a lot of pride in paying my employees well and making sure my family has everything they need. No, my cheapness extends only to myself. I'm not always as kind to myself as I am to others. I guess that's something else I need to work on.

Fortunately, even with getting lost, I still got to the Hollins home on time. In fact, dinner was still being cooked when I got there. I certainly don't expect my clients to feed me, so I made a mental note to knock this off of their bill. In fact, I could see that they were a family of relatively humble means and I resolved to charge them half of what I would normally charge someone for a case like this. I really didn't need the money, and a part of me felt dirty for even charging them half my usual rate. I really did just want to help them. Yes, business was good, so good that I'd recently added my friend

Randy to the roster as an additional investigator. He was taking over the other cases that had been on my plate so that I could devote all my attention to this matter. Even when business was slow, I had a dependable and generous additional source of income, although my pride prevented me from depending on that money too much. I tried to squirrel most of it away to help pay for my kids' college education somewhere down the road.

The weather was finally starting to get warm enough for grilling food outside, which is exactly what Greg Hollins was doing when I arrived. Cooking up a few steaks and veggies on the barbecue they kept on their back patio. Their house was in the Cape Cod style. While I was waiting for the food, Amanda gave me a quick tour of the house. She and Greg shared the single master bedroom downstairs, while the kids' bedrooms were all located upstairs along with another bathroom. A quick glance inside the bedrooms told me that they had hastily straightened up the house in anticipation of my arrival. I felt vaguely guilty about that. These people had more important things to worry about right now than trying to impress me.

I lingered when we reached Melissa's bedroom. It was messier than the other rooms. I'd asked them not to move anything inside it earlier. It was a little on the small side. A large bed dominated the room, a dresser and desk were crammed inside. Atop the prefabricated desk was the monitor for a PC, the graying off white CPU tower crammed beneath the desk, covered in a multitude of colorful stickers. The walls were filled with posters of things that had been popular around that time. Gwen Stefani and Blink 182, amongst others, all looking back at me while trying to look as cool as possible in their slick promo pics.

There were two windows in the room. One above her big, frilly pink four post bed and one located near the desk on the opposite wall. "Which of these windows was the one that you found opened that morning?" I needed to know.

"That one." She said sadly as she pointed to the one above the bed. I could tell that it was difficult for her to be in this room. He looked as if she was fighting to hold back her emotions. I'd decided I wouldn't stay there any longer than was necessary, I didn't want to be responsible for the poor woman having an embarrassing breakdown in front of a relative stranger.

I hurried over to the side of the bed. I noted that there was no screen on the window and that as Greg had already explained, it was impossible to open from the outside unless it was already unlocked. I also saw that there was a bit of an overhang from the roof directly below it. Below that overhang was another bit of roofing which covered the screened in sunroom on the back end of the house.

"It looks like someone could climb out of that window and make it to the ground pretty easily." I commented. I could easily picture someone as tiny as Melissa wriggling through that window.

"Yeah, we were worried about her doing that when we gave her this bedroom, but she never did. Or at least, we didn't think she did."

"You're sure she didn't bring anything with her? No money, no change of clothes or food?"

"Yeah, pretty sure."

I pulled a small digital camera out of the pocket of my trench coat and snapped a few pictures of the bedroom. I walked over to the desk with the computer on it and noticed a modem connected to it wedged between the wall and the monitor.

"This computer is connected to the web?"

"Yeah, we've got AOL. She uses it to research stuff for her school assignments." she said nonchalantly.

Once more, the alarms were sounding in my head. If she had online access, she could also be using the instant messenger that came with her service. There's no telling who she might've been talking to online. This is a danger that people are far more aware of nowadays than they were back then, when all of this stuff was still relatively new to the average American. Parental controls, if they existed at all, were even more of a joke than they are today, presenting virtually no challenge to a determined kid.

There's one way we can find out if she's been talking to anyone. I thought, remembering how good Penny was at figuring out what had been done on a computer.

"Is there any chance I can borrow this PC? I would only need to take the tower." I asked her.

"Yes, definitely! Do whatever might help." I could hear the desperation in her tone, and it broke my heart a little bit.

"Do you know if she kept a diary?"

"Not that I know of. Nothing that you'd call a proper diary. She does have a bunch of notebooks though, she likes to draw in them, and write little poems. Some of them are pretty good." Her voice broke, choked with feeling. She shoved it back down. "They're right over here, you're welcome to take those too, if you need to."

She indicated a small stack of those black and white covered composition notebooks that are so popular in grade schools which were sitting on a shelf jutting out of the wall above the desk.

"Thanks. I think I will take those too. Anything that can help me understand who she is might help me find her." As I said it, I dropped my camera back into my pocket and scooped up the stack of notebooks. I cradled them precariously in my arms.

I spotted a lone goldfish swimming in a bowl on Melissa's dresser, blissfully unaware of the family crisis unfolding around it. "What's the fish's name?"

"Goldie." Amanda answered with a slight smile.

I chuckled. "Kids! They're a real trip aren't they? We recently got a kitten for my daughter and you know what she wanted to name him? 'Kitty'! So original, huh? Kids love those incredibly literal names."

"That's precious! How old is she?" Amanda seemed grateful to have something to talk about other than her own woes for a change.

"Four."

"That's a great age, isn't it?" She asked wistfully.

"Yeah, but it sure can be a little challenging at times." I admitted. Sometimes my daughter Autumn did drive me nuts, but I knew that someday I'd miss what she was like at this age, just like I miss what my son Joe was like back then.

"So what did you end up naming the cat?"

"Methuselah." I revealed.

"Really?" She laughed for the first time since I'd met her. It was a wonderful sound.

"My wife's idea. She's a history professor and that was the name of the longest-lived man ever according to the Bible. She's hoping that naming the cat after him will give him a long life too." I explained.

This would turn out to be an ill-fated idea for naming a cat, as Methuselah would only last a few years before he ran off and was never seen again. Although I prefer to believe that he's still out there somewhere, now being hailed as a respected elder sage amongst his fellow felines. These days we have a different cat, the equally portentously named Zarathustra (named after an ancient Iranian prophet) whom we've had much better luck with. I really shouldn't let Naomi name our pets! Then again, when it's left up to me, I tend to give them uninspired, vanilla sounding names like 'Mike' which is our dog's moniker. Oh well, at least it's better than calling him 'doggie'.

"Dinner's ready!" Greg's voice called from somewhere below us.

We made our way out of the bedroom and down the stairs. As I walked, I spied a photo of a younger Greg decked out in a USMC dress uniform hanging on the wall beside me. I grinned faintly at this evidence that my guess at his military background had proven correct. I quickly located my briefcase, which I'd left sitting near the coffee table in their living room. I entered the combination that unlocked it and tried to fit the stack of Melissa's notebooks inside. It was a tight fit. My briefcase didn't hold as much as it looked like it could since it had a concealed compartment that held a special object I was tasked with guarding. Guarding this unusual object is the source of my extra income, and another consequence of my first adventure. The hidden compartment took up most of the space in the case, which irritatingly didn't leave much room for other things. I struggled to arrange the notebooks in such a way that would allow me to actually close it. It was a pain in the ass, but in the end, I succeeded.

After my battle with the briefcase, I joined the rest of the family at the dinner table in the small dining room that was just off of the kitchen. Greg already had everything for the meal laid out. The steaks he'd grilled were stacked on one plate, the veggies on another, and a large red plastic bowl held the salad Amanda had prepared. The other kids were already at the table. Ty looked to be around eight or nine years old. He was tall for his age and thin with a large, unruly mop of curly hair. Seated next to him was Dawn, who wasn't much taller than her brother despite being, at the age of 15, the oldest child in the family. She was also much more fair skinned than either of her siblings, with dirty blonde hair tied back into a ponytail. I would later discover that she looked so different from her brother and sister because she had a different biological father from Melissa and Ty, who Amanda had with Greg. My own family is a blended one. My son Joe also has a different biological father who had so little interest in the boy that he didn't seem to care when I adopted him shortly after marrying Naomi. I've never really understood how someone can possibly have such a disinterested attitude towards their own flesh and blood.

The food was delicious, but then again, I'm pretty easy to please when it comes to eating, despite what anyone else might tell you. The dinner was a little surreal at times, with everyone trying to pretend that they were still a normal family. The chair that Melissa would've filled in happier times yawned mockingly at them with its emptiness. I felt like an intruder being there in their home during this difficult time despite all their attempts to make me feel welcome. I felt like I had no business being here, bearing witness to their carefully concealed grief.

I brought them all up to speed on my investigation thus far. I could tell that Greg was obviously perturbed that I was treating this like a case of her running away from home when he clearly believed that she had snuck out with the intention of returning only to meet with foul play. Even though this was an ugly scenario, in some ways I think it was easier for him to face than the idea that anything in her home life had been so unpleasant that she'd want to escape from it. I tried to calm him down by assuring him that I was just being thorough, that I had to look into every possibility. This seemed to do the trick, and his anxieties were soon assuaged.

After finishing dinner, I got permission to talk to the kids. I spoke to them at the dinner table, one at a time, without either of their parents present, although Amanda was in the kitchen nearby the entire time. Greg had left the house with a group of concerned neighbors and friends to canvas the neighborhood passing out flyers with her picture on them. He had taken the past week off of work and this was how he spent the majority of his days lately.

I wanted the kids to feel comfortable telling me anything that they might not want to disclose in front of their parents. Unfortunately, I didn't really learn much of any value from them, aside from getting a few insights into their individual relationships with Melissa. Despite the fact that they attended the same school, Dawn and Melissa moved in very different circles, and seemed to exist in different worlds. I got the impression that Dawn was more popular, a preppy cheerleader who had little time for her more withdrawn and artistically inclined little sister. Nonetheless, she was obviously as upset about her sister's disappearance as her parents were. Sadly, she was also as clueless about it as they were. From Dawn I discovered that Melissa was the peacekeeper of the family, who was obsessed with making sure that everyone was being treated fairly. She also had a bit of a bad temper that could erupt at unpredictable times. I didn't find this terribly surprising. Much of it was typical middle child behavior. As an only child, it wasn't something I had any firsthand experience of, but I'd read up on it.

Having a decent understanding of other people's psychology was essential for being a competent detective.

Ty was obviously closer to Melissa. She had a protective attitude towards him and played with him the most. Although it appeared that lately she'd seemed distracted by something and hadn't made as much time for him as she usually did. He complained that she was always holed up in her room, on her computer. What she was doing on the computer, he really couldn't say for sure. He thought maybe she was playing a game.

I did get a few more details about Melissa's friends from her siblings, but nothing truly significant. Her parents had already provided me with a list of them with their contact information, which I had requested from them. Getting in touch with them was part of my game plan for tomorrow's phase of the investigation. Talking to Melissa's siblings gave me a better idea of how to prioritize which of her friends to talk to first, who she spent the most time with and was closest to. Having exhausted my list of questions, I flipped shut the small notepad I always kept on me, tucking it and my trusty mechanical pencil into a pocket. It was getting late and I'd learned about as much as I figured I could learn at the house tonight. I went back up to Melissa's bedroom and unplugged her CPU, collected my briefcase, and said my goodbyes. Amanda insisted on carrying the bulky CPU out to my car. I popped the trunk open and placed it carefully on its side along with my briefcase. Amanda's eyes fixated on a long, black case that was also stored in the trunk.

"What's that? Are you carrying a rocket launcher around in your trunk?" She joked.

"Something like that." I smiled back mysteriously. What the case contained was actually the *Vermilion Avenger*, the same sword that typically hung on the wall of my office. I brought it with me whenever I was guarding the object I kept in my briefcase.

Perhaps she sensed that she wasn't going to get any more answers out of me on the topic, because she didn't press the matter. "I'll bring back all of Melissa's things once I've gotten whatever information I might need out of them." I promised her, not that she appeared to be overly concerned with such questions.

I spent a little time driving up and down the suburban streets of Raritan myself before heading back home, trying to familiarize myself with Melissa's world. I saw Greg and his small search party on one of the blocks and gave him a small wave. As I gazed out at the houses, with their windows staring back at me vacantly, I wished they could speak to me, that they could somehow be forced to give up the secret of whatever they might have borne witness to four nights earlier.

Even though Raritan isn't very far away from where I live, the drive back felt longer than it really was somehow. My mind was constantly churning over the details of the case, struggling to find answers during the entire trip.

I arrived back at my home in North Brunswick well past nine at night. As usual, I was serenaded by the strident barks of my golden retriever, Mike, as I walked up the front steps. Once inside, he almost knocked me over with the enthusiasm of his customary greeting. The only thing that kept me on my feet was the counterbalance of the weight of the case holding the *Vermilion Avenger* that I held in one hand.

"Jesus, Mike, take a chill pill!" I admonished him, but he wouldn't relent until I set down my briefcase that was in my other hand and rubbed the top of his head with the proper vigor. Placated for the moment, the dog skulked down the short flight of stairs to my left that led to the lower part of our home, where he reigned as king. I picked up my briefcase again and continued on beyond the foyer. As I walked past our den, I saw the top of Joe's head, the rest of him concealed by the couch he was on. The TV blared out a particularly loud and obnoxious local commercial in front of him.

"Hey, Matt!" He called out to me. He usually called me by my first name instead of 'Dad' since I hadn't been his dad when we first met. I was used to it, but sometimes it bugged me a little. At least I had Autumn to fulfill my apparent need to be addressed by my proper parental title.

"Hey yourself, kiddo! Did you have a good day today?"

"It was a day." He answered neutrally, but truthfully, which was the important thing. I couldn't stand insincere small talk and people pretending to be okay when they really weren't. This was especially true after spending the last few hours in a house where everyone was intent on doing just that.

"Yeah, me too." I replied. It was the most succinct way to summarize the swirl of conflicting emotions welling up within me: excitement to have a new case, one that I felt really mattered, tinged with sadness over how Melissa's disappearance was affecting her family and anxiety about my ability to bring about a positive outcome for them all. There was something more. This case was a reminder of how fragile my own family situation was–of how vulnerable we all are. It was a grim reminder that tragedy could strike at any minute, tearing away our illusion of stability and normality. It's the ugly truth about existence that we spend most of our time distracting ourselves from for the sake of our own sanity. When seen from this perspective, even the most mundane of interactions with someone we care about suddenly becomes something impossibly precious, something we might never get to experience again. I was doubly determined not to take the people that I cared about the most for granted after the day I'd just had.

"Is that my man I hear? It's about time you showed up!" Naomi asked from the dining room table.

I ambled over to where she sat, hunched over the table which was a mess of various stacks of papers spread out so evenly that they obscured its surface. Many of the papers were photocopies of old manuscripts, or typed up translations of ones that weren't in English. Directly in front of Naomi was a legal notepad and a tall glass of wine. She tilted her head up at me and smiled. She was as beautiful as ever, petite and curvaceous with dark olive skin, equally dark hair and glittering light brown eyes that were almost golden. How I longed to disappear into that smile and all that it promised, to lose myself and bury all of my worries in her arms. But she was busy, so instead I just leaned down and kissed her on the cheek.

"I see you got another delivery today." I noted nodding my head in the direction of the papers filling up the table.

"Yeah. It's all the records from the Temple of the Old Gods from the 1700's. Well, the first box load of them at least!" She couldn't conceal the excitement in her voice. For her, getting her hands on these records was like opening up a bunch of Christmas presents. It warmed my heart to see her so happy. I'm obsessed with solving the mysteries of the present, whereas she was consumed with unraveling the secrets of the distant past. Was it any wonder that we were married?

The Temple of the Old Gods was a secret society of mystics, one of the most important groups in the Guilds, which was a kind of alliance of secret societies. I had stumbled across their existence years earlier, while working a different missing person's case. We'd befriended some of the leaders of the Guilds during the course of that case and Naomi had talked them into making her their head archivist. In her spare time, she was working on writing a comprehensive history of the world that incorporated the role of the Guilds in shaping our history. It was a monumental task. She planned on calling this work the *Magna Historia Mundi*, which was just "the Great History of the World" in Latin. My wife delights in giving everything overly grandiose titles. She knew that her pet project would never be read by anyone outside of the Guilds, but she didn't particularly care. She was doing it more to satisfy her own curiosity than for any other reason.

We received regular shipments of records from the various Guilds. The bottom level of our house, where Naomi's home office was located, was filled with them. She preferred to work at the dining room table though, where she could keep an eye on the kids.

"Where's that daughter of mine at?" I inquired.

"Right where she should be at this time of night, in her room, pretending to be asleep, duh!" She looked at me quizzically, as if sizing me up. In fact, that's exactly what she was doing. She could always see right through me.

"This new case with the missing little girl is already starting to get to you, isn't it?"

I shrugged, trying to look nonchalant and fooling nobody. "Maybe a little. Let's just say that it's making me realize I'm lucky I am to have the kids in my life. Hell, I'm even grateful that you're still hanging around to make our dining room table so cluttered and nonfunctional."

"Careful, Spike! You might just charm me out of my pants with such smooth, romantic talk! As far as this table goes, I'd argue that it's *very* functional. It's doing an outstanding job of containing my research in my humble opinion."

I couldn't argue with that. And at least she didn't deny that it was cluttered.

"I'm gonna go up and kiss our very safe and secure daughter goodnight while I still can." I announced as I started to set down my briefcase and the long case holding the *Vermilion Avenger* on the table.

"Hey! Don't put that stuff on top of my papers!" Naomi protested. "You know where those things belong!" She pointed in the direction of my own home office imperiously. "This might look like nothing but a disorganized mess to you, but I assure you that these papers are all arranged in a very particular order that only I can decipher! I can't have you screwing up my system."

"System! Yeah, right! Tell me another one, Professor!" I mockingly complained as I hefted my dual cases back up from the table.

"Don't argue with me, pal! You can't possibly win–I have more letters after my name than you do, PI!" She playfully fought back.

"Elitist!" I accused as I shuffled off towards my office.

I heard her blow a raspberry my way as I flipped on the light with my elbow. I grinned at our silly banter.

I set the burdensome cases on my own desk, which was refreshingly blank in comparison to Naomi's workspace. The only other thing on my desk was my own PC and a mug full of pens and pencils. I opened the case that held the *Vermilion Avenger*. It floated inside of it. Yes, I said it floated. Here's where things start to get a little weird. This particular sword is made of very exotic materials. It's very dense and too heavy to be lifted. So it floats in midair. It's made of stuff that can defy gravity, and which is also responsive to thoughts. Yes, I know how crazy this all sounds.

In my mind, I envisioned the sword to rise up out of its case and fly over to the suit of somewhat futuristic armor which stood on a short pedestal in the opposite corner. No sooner had I imagined it than it happened in reality. The sword whooshed past me and planted itself in the hands of the armored suit so that it was pointing downwards, with the point resting in a deep groove between the feet of the armor. Both the uncanny sword and the armor had come from our friends in the Guilds. It was all special equipment given to us to help Naomi and I guard what was hidden inside the secret compartment in my briefcase. I now opened that briefcase, first removing Melissa's notebooks, then pressing my thumb against a metal plate which made the compartment pop open. Inside, cushioned by a gray foam lining was the object. It was called the Orb of Sinister.

Just looking at it, it was singularly unimpressive. For one thing, it didn't look like any kind of orb. It wasn't a sphere. It was in the form of a cheap looking plastic statue of a boy in blue shorts wearing a bright yellow jacket and a purple baseball cap. This was an illusion as the Orb could take different forms to disguise itself. You see, the Orb is a magic item.

Yes, magic is real, a concept I still find hard to accept despite the fact that evidence of its reality is always within easy reach of me. Hell, my friend and partner Randy is even a card-carrying wizard in the Temple of the Old Gods, the most powerful group of magic users on the planet. The purpose of the Orb is to prevent magic spells from being cast.

It instantly cancels out any new spells that are cast in a radius of roughly 10 miles around it. It's possibly the only thing that prevents those who know how to use magic from completely dominating the world and subjugating us normal folks. When the Orb is near, even the most formidable of wizards or witches are as vulnerable as the rest of us. It's the only thing that can level the playing field. The Orb of Sinister is a copy of a more ancient Orb called the Orb of Thoth. For centuries that Orb was guarded by a cult of assassins and their successors. The threat that they might use it kept the peace–until it was stolen and shot into space by some wizards that were up to no good.

Our friends in the Guilds entrusted Naomi and I with guarding this new Orb so that it couldn't be stolen and disposed of like that ever again. Very few people knew that the Orb existed, even fewer knew that it was kept by some random PI and his college professor wife. It was still a dangerous job, but we were well paid for it. Naomi and I took turns, alternating our days taking care of it. When it wasn't with me, she kept it in a safe in her office at the university where she worked. The *Vermilion Avenger* also hung on her walls as a 'decoration' on those occasions. Only a thought away from her side should danger present itself. Thankfully it seldom did. In the years since we'd served as 'Guardians of the Orb', there had only been one time when someone had tried to take it from us. There's a little tracking device attached to the Orb, so that even if someone did get it, there's a good chance it could be recovered.

There was a painting of King Arthur on the wall behind my desk. It was attached to the wall in such a way that it could easily swing out, revealing a hidden safe, which I now opened. Doing this little routine always made me feel like a secret agent. In my office at work I had an identical safe that was concealed by a tapestry of a dragon. Next, I picked up a pair of tongs that I also kept in the briefcase. I used this to remove the Orb and transfer it to the safe, which I then sealed shut and moved the painting back into place. The tongs weren't really necessary. One could touch the Orb, but doing so was a very unpleasant experience. The Orb was powered by hundreds of souls that were trapped inside. When your skin made contact with its surface, you could *feel* them inside, calling to you. It's an impossibly eerie sensation that's difficult to describe and one that I feel is best to avoid. I don't like those spooky vibes that it gives off at all, hence the tongs.

Now that this little ritual was completed, I could finally go check on my daughter. I left the light on in my home office since I planned to return there to go over Melissa's notebooks later on. I walked past Naomi, still happily hunched over the table, sorting out her historical puzzles and headed up the long flight of stairs that led to the second story of our house.

When I reached the top, I made my way down the hall to Autumn's bedroom and spied its door, already partially cracked open. I peered inside and by the dim light of her nightlight I could see her lying in the bed, Methuselah the kitten curled up at her feet. I swung the door open just wide enough to slip through sideways and crept inside. I'm a pretty tall guy, so I had to duck my head slightly as I entered.

I leaned over her, brushed some of the brown hair from her forehead and kissed it. She smiled, her eyes fluttering open.

"Faker!" I accused playfully.

"Hello, Daddy."

"Goodnight, daughter." I said firmly.

I stroked the kitty as I passed him and made for the door. I lingered there on the threshold for a few moments, grateful that I knew where my daughter was right now, being all too painfully aware of those who had lost this most basic level of security in their lives. Perhaps that was something I could give back to them? I had to dare to hope that I was up to the task.

I made my way back down to my office, pausing to appreciate the fact that I also knew where Joe was. I was reminded of something that used to play on TV when I was a kid: sometimes an announcer's voice would come on between commercials and say in a grave voice "It's nine o'clock, so you know where your children are?" Well, Mr. Announcer Man, I did indeed know where they were, and I prayed that I'd never take that fact for granted again.

I settled down into the chair behind my desk (thankfully it wasn't as squeaky as the one at work) and started thumbing through Melissa's notebooks. Fortunately, some of the entries and drawings had dates on them, which made it easier for me to sort them into something resembling chronological order. I felt a little strange going through her private notes like this. I'm a big believer in everyone's right to privacy, yet the irony is that as a PI, in various ways I have to constantly violate that right as part of my job. It's a paradox that I wrestle with at times. In this case, I knew it was for a very good cause, so I dismissed such ideas from the forefront of my mind. If anything, I learned in these notebooks helped bring Melissa back home safely, it was worth the price of temporarily stripping away her privacy. The end justifies the means. Her right to privacy was a luxury she couldn't afford right now.

I spent hours reading over Melissa's notebooks, losing all track of time. The only reminder of the world outside was when Naomi yelled at Joe to tell him to go to bed. The only thing harder than getting that kid out of bed was getting him into it in the first place.

Eventually, Naomi wandered into the office. I didn't even hear her come in.

"You should come to bed, it's late." She said from next to my chair making me nearly jump out of my skin. She giggled and put her hand up to her mouth to hide her smile when she saw how I reacted.

"Holy shit! You scared the fuck out of me!"

"That must be some truly engrossing stuff you're reading there if you didn't hear my fat ass waddle in here." She smirked sarcastically.

"Hey! That's no way to talk about that perfectly proportioned derrière that I can't get enough of!" I said as I gave it an appreciative smack.

"Ah, you always know exactly the right thing to say, don't you?" She laughed.

"I try, Lord knows I try."

"So what is all this stuff that's succeeded in so completely captivating your attention?" She waved a hand towards the stack of notebooks.

"Journals that belonged to the missing kid, Melissa. Closest thing she had to a diary. The kid is actually a pretty good writer, and not half a bad artist either." I informed her. Of course, for anyone to qualify as being 'not half a bad artist' in my book, they have to be able to draw something slightly above the level of a stick figure, which is my own highest level of drawing ability. As a writer though, I like to think that my literary critiques carry a bit more weight.

"Oh? Is that your professional opinion, oh great author?"

"It is. She's got a real way with words. It's much more sophisticated than the usual teen angst. Way better than the crap I used to fill my notebooks with at that age."

Naomi laughed. "Yeah, that stuff *was* pretty awful!"

"Hey! When did you ever read any of that?"

"Some of it got published in our High School literary journal, remember? Honestly, I think the participation was so low they'd print anything!"

"Omigod! Visions!" Visions was the name of the creative writing collection our school published once a year. "I forgot all about that!" I was mortified to realize that Naomi had read anything of mine that was ever published there.

"Don't look so sad. I didn't fall in love with you because of your writing ability– which *has* improved, by the way."

"Well anyway, like I was saying, this kid really had talent." I reiterated, desperate to steer the subject away from the literary sins of my past.

"*Has* talent. Not had. She's still out there, and you're gonna find her." Naomi said pointedly.

"God, I hope so." I was touched by her confidence in me, especially since too often I didn't share it.

"So has anything in those books helped you figure anything out yet?" She asked. I was grateful for her interest. Years earlier, before she finished getting her degree, Naomi used to do Penny's job for me. I missed bouncing my ideas off of her and getting her insights into my cases. I don't mind admitting that she's smarter than I am, it's part of what makes her so damned sexy to me. She usually points me in the right direction–so long as I'm humble enough to actually take her advice.

"It's helping me understand her better. Who she is as a person. I'm seeing a few recurring themes in these poems and her other scribblings. An overwhelming sense of loneliness, a feeling that nobody understands her or ever will. There's also lots of fear about the future, of having to be out on her own and never finding anyone else to share her life with. I'm thinking that as a middle child, she felt overlooked by her parents and this fed into all those feelings, making them even more intense. I'm worried that all of this might've made her extra vulnerable to anyone she might've met who showed her any attention."

"That's what you think happened? She ran off with some guy?"

"Or girl. Ya never know." I reminded her.

"That's true enough." She allowed.

"She had a computer in her bedroom. You know how pedophiles are starting to use the internet to target kids these days? I'm afraid that something like that might've happened to her. She didn't take any money or clothes with her, maybe she expected someone else to provide all of that for her? Someone older, someone with more resources?"

"She didn't even bring a change of underwear?" Naomi shook her head in disbelief.

"Nope."

"That is a little odd - and gross." She admitted.

"Granted, she didn't have a job, so she didn't have much money to begin with, just a few dollars from her allowance. It wouldn't have gotten her very far even if she had brought it. Of course, she might've just gone out with the intention of coming right back and some random creep grabbed her off the street. That's what her Dad thinks. However, that sort of thing is rare. Usually, missing kids know the person they go off with, especially older ones like her. I mean, how many years now have we been warning kids about 'stranger danger'? By now they've got the memo and Melissa is no dummy. Either way, I'm afraid it doesn't look that good for her. Even though she's only been gone for a few days, statistically the chances of finding her are already pretty shitty and getting shittier every day."

"You're really worried about her, aren't you?"

"Yeah. Reading through these notebooks makes me feel pretty close to her, like I can see who she really is inside. She has so much talent, so much potential, so much to offer the world! I hate to see that go to waste. At the same time, she's also terribly fragile. She's wise beyond her years in lots of ways, but at the end of the day she's still just a clueless kid. It's a fucked up world out there, full of fucked up people. It chews up and spits out sensitive people like her every day." I confessed.

"If you're really that concerned about it, maybe you should call the ABC?" She suggested.

The ABC was a part of the Guilds. Their main job was covering up evidence of the Guilds' activities. They were the real life basis for all the stories about people being questioned by mysterious "Men in Black" after something strange has just happened. Agent Dale, the leader of the local branch, was always trying to convince me to join them. In a way, he had already recruited me, albeit unofficially. He sometimes hired my detective agency to do surveillance and other small jobs for them when he claimed that he was understaffed. I took the jobs, their money was as green as anyone else's wasn't it? I tried to treat them like any other clients even though they were far more than that.

"No way! That's not necessary! I can solve this on my own. It's just a routine missing persons case. I took her computer and Penny's going to go through it tomorrow looking for clues. I'm sure she'll find something useful, she always does. Anyway, weren't you the one who was just saying that you believed I'd find her?"

"I don't doubt your ability, it's just that the ABC has lots of really advanced technology and other abilities that we don't have. It's obvious that you're starting to get really attached to this girl. All I'm saying is that if she's really in danger, getting some help from the ABC could really speed things up and get her to safety before it's too late. I'm sure if you asked Agent Dale he'd be happy to..."

"No! I don't want to go running to them every time we have a problem." I cut her off, sounding far harsher than I had meant to. I immediately regretted it. She didn't deserve to be talked to like that, she was just trying to help.

"I'm sorry. I didn't mean to snap at you. It's just...well you know how I feel about trying to keep my distance from all that weird Guild shit. I just wanna have a normal life sometimes, ya know?"

She smiled at me. "It's too late for that, don't you think, mighty Guardian of the Orb?"

"Sometimes I wish we'd never accepted that damned job." It was true. The existence of the Guilds, the reality of magic– all the things I'd learned about the true nature of reality, it was all a bit too much for me to handle sometimes. It left me with a serious case of the existential blues. Naomi had a different attitude, her studies of the histories of the Guilds had led her to believe that they were a mostly positive force in the world, that civilization would have perished several times without them. But for me, it was sometimes hard to see them as anything other than a (barely) necessary evil. My association with them often made me feel tainted somehow. I often wondered what the human race might've achieved without their sometimes heavy handed influence? There were plenty of good people in the Guilds, but also lots of bad ones that were mixed up in some pretty questionable things. Only an idiot would trust them completely.

She squeezed my hand. "I know, but we *did* agree to it and now we have to live with the consequences of that decision. Besides, 'that damned job' paid for this nice, big house and is gonna put our kids through college someday. Look, why not take advantage of the positives in our situation? We have strong connections to some of the most powerful, resourceful people and organizations on the entire planet–why not use that every once in a while? You'd better believe that if it was one of our own kids that was in danger, I'd be pulling out all the stops and calling in every favor!" I didn't doubt it. You didn't want to mess with Naomi when she was in 'mama bear' mode.

"Yeah, but it's *not* one of our kids, is it? And I don't need the ABC to solve my cases for me. I was hired to do a job and I'm gonna get it done without them."

She sighed and shook her head at my supreme pig headedness. She knew better than to try and argue with me when I got like this. Instead, she just said "I'll see you upstairs in a few," with an uncharacteristic resignation in her voice.

That night I did not sleep well. I had a series of nightmares, but I couldn't remember any of the details outside of one disturbing image that was still stuck in my mind the next morning. An image of Melissa Hollins staring up at me from the bottom of a dark well, her skin ashen and all covered in bruises. Her eyes were lifeless, yet somehow still burned accusingly up at me. "Why weren't you fast enough?" they seemed to implore.

"Hang on! I'm coming! I'll save you!" I shouted as I ran forward, thrusting my hands into the dark pit to pull her out. But it was too late, the top of her head was already disappearing, submerging below the black, oily waters of the well, never to be seen again.

INVESTIGATION DAY TWO

The next day I struggled to carry Melissa's CPU up the steps and into my office. I was grateful that today was Naomi's day to guard the Orb, otherwise I would've had to make another trip back to my car to bring in the *Vermilion Avenger*. It was already hard enough to lug the bulky CPU tower through the door and carry my briefcase all at the same time. At times like that I often wished that I had an extra arm coming out of my side. As usual, Penny was already at the office ahead of me and had a hot pot of coffee already waiting for me in the kitchen. The heady smell of it teased my nostrils as I lumbered through the door.

"Hey, Penny!" I called out to her.

"Good morning, Boss." She droned without looking up at me. She kept a musical keyboard that she used to compose her music on one end of her desk in case inspiration should suddenly strike her, as it often did at odd times. She was jabbing at a few of its keys, hammering out part of a tune in a tinny, flat electronic tone. She frowned thoughtfully down at the alternating black and white keys, her sharply pointed, freckled nose wrinkling in frustration. Whatever muse had recently alighted upon her had obviously fled, maybe I'd scared it away with the clumsiness of my arrival?

I set the CPU down on Penny's desk, with a bit of a thump, despite my best efforts to be gentle with it.

She looked up at me with a look of mild annoyance flashing in her emerald eyes, which were perpetually ringed in heavy dark eyeliner. "Careful with that thing! You don't want to break it, do you?"

"It belongs to Mellisa Hollins. I need you to check it out, see if there's anything of interest on it."

"Yeah, I figured. Did you remember to get the password this time?" She asked somewhat wearily. Last time I'd asked her to do something like this for me I hadn't. She'd still been able to hack into that computer somehow, she had her ways, which frankly I know nothing about (all this hacker shit is beyond me). However, even so, not having the password had slowed her down considerably, annoying her to no end. She whined about it at every opportunity. I didn't really mind. It was all part of the daily dance we performed with each other. A lot of our relationship consisted of us constantly 'busting each other's balls' as my Dad would say. Underneath all the ribbing, we had a deep respect for one another.

"Yup! I had her mom write it down and tape it to it. It's right there." I tapped on a haphazardly torn strip of lined notebook paper taped next to the power button with perhaps a touch too much pride that I'd remembered how to avoid Penny's wrath this time.

"Anything in particular I should be looking for on this dinosaur?" She asked as she eyed the outdated, hand me down computer with thinly disguised skepticism.

"I trust your instincts, just look for anything unusual. You know, anything that seems suspicious for a thirteen-year-old girl to have on her computer." I thought my show of confidence in her would satisfy her, but I was wrong. Penny is a very detail oriented person who likes specifics.

"Okay...kinda vague." She complained.

"Worst case scenario: I'm afraid that she might've been using this to chat with older guys. Especially keep an eye out for anything like that." I clarified. I assume that satiated her, as she finally smiled back at me.

"Your flagon of magic elixir awaits you, Sire." She waved a hand in the direction of the kitchen.

"I know, I could smell that divine aroma as soon as I walked in, thanks." I grinned back at her like an addict about to get his fix, which I suppose I am.

She shrugged. "It's what I do." I saw her pull the CPU closer to her and begin hooking it up to her own computer's keyboard and monitor as I slipped into the small kitchen area off to the side of her desk.

I quickly located my favorite mug from the drying rack, emblazoned with the legend "World's Greatest Dick" (Naomi's idea of a joke) and filled it with coffee. This was actually my second cup of the morning since I usually had one before leaving the house. Doubtlessly, I'd be pissing up a storm in the near future–coffee is after all, a highly effective diuretic. Yet, a few extra trips to the bathroom was a small price to pay for the clarity of mind that it buys me, as its glorious dark waters dissolve away the clinging cobwebs left over from my dreams. Or in this case, nightmares. The unsettling images from the previous night's fitful sleep still tortured me whenever I turned my mind towards them, so I made a point not to do so.

Coffee securely in hand now, I made my way into my office. I decided I would start the day with the tedious task of reviewing the copy of the security tape from the train station. I would definitely need all the coffee I could get to keep myself from passing out while watching such dull fare. I had an old TV/VCR combo that had faithfully served me for years tucked into a shelf on the wall opposite my desk. I retrieved the tape from my briefcase and popped it in to begin my exciting morning viewing session. This is how I planned to occupy my time until it got closer to two pm, when the kids from Melissa's school got out. I had a small list of her friends that I hoped to interview later on today. I took a break for lunch around eleven thirty as I usually did, then returned to watching something that would've been perfect for a TV show called "America's Dullest Videos".

The video tape was a complete dead end. Melissa never showed up on it. I wasn't surprised. I'd already suspected that this angle wouldn't pan out. I turned to the list of her friends Melissa's folks had provided along with contact numbers for their respective parents. I'd made notes in the margins after speaking with Melissa's siblings ranking the friends in order of who seemed to be closest to her. I'd ranked Erica Suarez at the top of that list. I picked up the receiver on my desktop phone to dial her parents' number to arrange for an interview when there was a familiarly sheepish knock at my door. I immediately knew who it was and dropped the receiver back on its cradle.

"Come in Randy."

The door swung open to reveal my partner, Randy Grumman. He was a tall, young man in his early twenties with a generous pompadour of unruly, wavy dark hair, topping a round, cherubic face currently filled with stubble from the beard he was trying to grow. A pair of thick glasses distorted the proportions of his eyes enlarging them comically.

"What's up?" I inquired casually as he shuffled into the room uncertainly.

"I was just thinking that maybe you could use a little *special* help on this case you're working on?"

"Special help? Like what kind of 'special help'?" I asked, although I already had a pretty good idea of what he meant.

"You know, the magical kind? Like, I could do a tracer spell for you for example?" Randy was a member of the Temple of the Old Gods and therefore a wizard. He wasn't just any old wizard either. He'd been personally recruited and trained by their leader, Wendy Sommardahl. Despite his youth, he was already considered to be one of the best magic users on the planet. Many people saw him as a shoo in to replace Wendy someday as leader of that secret group of mages. I hoped that wouldn't happen any time soon. I needed him right where he was now, helping me out. For his part, Randy seemed perfectly content to work as a PI and play bass in his band. If he had any ambitions of inheriting Wendy's position, he was sure doing a great job of hiding it from everyone.

"Pal, you know that I have no idea what the hell a 'tracer spell' is." I informed him.

"Well, if you took me to this girl's house and I got a hold of something that she used a lot recently–or possibly even a part of her, like one of her hairs from her brush I could do the spell. It does exactly what it sounds like it does. It creates a path that traces her most recent movements that only the spellcaster can see. The problem is that it doesn't have a very long range, only a few miles. So if she's not still somewhere nearby we'll lose the trail, but even if that happens at least it'll give us an idea of what path she took and the right direction to start searching in." He rapidly and excitedly over-explained, as was his habit once he got rolling on a topic he was knowledgeable about–which was most topics.

I sighed loudly, on purpose for dramatic effect. "Naomi put you up to asking about this didn't she?"

"No..." he began, then looked down and said "...yes." The kid was always so earnest and lacking in guile. Lying never came easy to him. It was one of the things I loved best about him as a person, and why I trusted him with being my partner, even if a total lack of a poker face was something of a liability for a private eye.

"I knew it! I knew she wouldn't just let this go!"

"Matt, don't be mad at her, she's just worried about you, and after talking to her, I am too." He said more forcefully, looking up at me, meeting my eyes for the first time.

"Why is everyone so worried about me all of the sudden? This is just another missing persons case, I've worked a few of them before in the past, as you well know. I'm more than capable of solving one without the help of the ABC or resorting to using magic! That's like... like... cheating! I like to do things the old fashioned way whenever possible, you know that!" I couldn't keep the frustration out of my voice.

"Yeah, but we all know that these missing person cases usually don't turn out so well. Most of the time, they turn up dead, or we find out that they've run off to be with a secret lover and aren't ever planning on coming back, or we can't find them at all. Besides, this is the first one you've ever worked on that involved someone so young." He argued back.

"So what? There's a minor involved. That doesn't really change anything."

"Naomi doesn't think so and she's got a point. We all know how personally you take some of these cases. You're so protective of your own kids, what'll happen to you if you can't save someone else's kid? I just want to do whatever I can to make sure this case has a good outcome for everyone involved–the clients and the investigator. If that means using a little magic, then so be it."

"You wanna know what you can do to help me? Take care of all the other cases I put on the back burner so I could devote all my energy to solving this one like I asked you to! I don't need any magic. Sherlock Holmes didn't need any magic!" I shot back.

Randy looked at me sadly. "Matt, you're a smart guy, but with all due respect, you're no Sherlock. I'm just saying that we should use all the tools in our toolbox if a kid's wellbeing is in danger."

I wondered if maybe I was pushing him too far. A part of me worried that he was making a good point, and I was just being too damned proud and stubborn to admit it. "Just do what I asked you to do, okay? I'll think about what you said. If I have a change of heart, I'll let you know, alright?" I said in a calmer voice.

Randy spread out his long fingers, calloused from hours spent playing bass guitar in the band he was in with Penny, in a gesture of surrender. "That's all I ask. Please let me know if there's anything else I can do for you."

"Thanks, pal. I will. I appreciate it, really I do, you're a good friend."

He beamed back at me as he turned to leave the room. Randy looked up to me and his ego was relatively easy to stroke. I had meant what I said about him being a good friend, but mostly I said it to get him out of my hair. I imagine that for his part, Randy also felt some satisfaction with planting the seeds of the idea of using magic to find Melissa in my mind. He knew that I was a creature of habit, and new ideas had to be slowly introduced to me before I eventually surrendered to them. No doubt he had high hopes that I'd come around to his point of view in time.

It wasn't totally out of the question either. I hadn't known that Randy could perform a spell like the one he'd described to me. The idea of asking him for help was far less humiliating to me than that of crawling to the Guilds and begging for their assistance. Still, the idea of resorting to using magic made my skin crawl. I tried my best to pretend that I still lived in a completely rational world where that sort of thing only existed where it couldn't hurt anyone, that it stayed where it belonged– in fantasy stories. My life was already weird enough.

Yet I couldn't deny the logic that it would be careless of me not to make use of his magic if I didn't develop any solid leads soon. Here I was, on day two of my investigation and I felt like I was still just treading water. All I had was a half-baked theory with no real evidence for it. This was day *five* for Melissa. Where was she right now? What was she doing? Most importantly, was she safe? Her dead eyes still haunted me from my nightmare. The words *"Why weren't you fast enough?"* still rang in my ears. Yes, I owed it to her to do everything possible to bring her back home alive. I resolved right then and there to do so–even if it meant using magic, but only if I felt like I still wasn't getting anywhere after today.

I picked up the phone again, then paused. I was unable to recall exactly who I'd been about to call before Randy had interrupted me.

"Now where the fuck was I?" I asked the room, but it just echoed my words back at me mockingly. Then I looked down at the papers in front of me and saw the number for Erica's parents.

"Oh yeah." At least there was one mystery I was still capable of solving on my own!

I dialed the number and arranged to meet with them around four-thirty pm. Erica's Mom would be home from work by then.

I still had some time to kill between when the kids started getting out of school and my meeting with Erica, so I set up one more meeting with another of Melissa's friends to fill the time in between. That left only one other friend on the list to talk to. I wasn't able to reach their parents, but I left a message on their voicemail asking for a call back to my cell number. With any luck, I'd be able to talk to all three of her closest friends before the day was out.

One thing was for sure–I wouldn't find any more answers here, cooped up in this office. It was time for me to get back out on the streets. My conversation with Randy had lit a fire under my ass, renewing my determination to finally get somewhere with this case–if only to avoid the deadline I'd set for myself before I'd have to resort to using more occult methods to get results.

On my way out, I asked Penny how she was getting along with the job I'd tasked her with.

"There wasn't anything interesting under the main profile on this thing. Mostly papers she wrote for school and some video games. However, I just found a hidden profile on here that I've been trying to get into."

"A hidden profile, huh? Wow! That's something!"

"Yeah the girl's pretty slick. Looks like she had something to hide after all."

I didn't know how to feel about this latest development. On the one hand, it suggested that I was likely on the right track, that she was indeed concealing things from her parents. If I could discover what those things were, I might finally start getting somewhere with this case. On the other hand, I was afraid to find out exactly *what* those secrets might be. I was terrified that my worst suspicions about this case might turn out to be eerily on the nose. Sometimes, it's much better to be wrong. I hoped that Melissa had simply run away from home in a temporary pique of teenage angst in the hopes of finally getting some attention from her parents. Maybe I'd find her hiding out in some abandoned building somewhere in her town? Yet my gut kept telling me that something more sinister might have befallen her instead.

Penny continued, "The problem is that it's proving pretty hard to get into that profile. I was wondering if you could let me take a look at her notebooks? They might give me a better idea of what she's using for a password."

"What? Is that really necessary? I thought you had some kinda fancy hacker software to help you get around passwords?"

"I do, but that shit takes forever to run, especially on an old pile of junk like this. That's why I get a little pissed when you hand me something like this and expect results right away. I think it's sweet that you think I'm some kind of a whiz with computers, but I'm really not." She said with an uncharacteristic petulance.

Usually Penny behaved as if she could take on anything. She liked to make a show of being a tough punk rock girl and often didn't let her vulnerabilities show like this in her daily interactions. She saved such feelings for her songs, oddly feeling more comfortable sharing that part of herself on a stage in front of a bunch of strangers than she sometimes did with her closest friends.

"Well, you sure as hell know more about them than I do!" I tried to restore her flagging confidence as best I could. It was obvious that she was feeling frustrated from her recent efforts.

She gave me a withering look. "Matt, even your mom knows more about computers than you do!"

I chuckled. "Yeah, that's probably true." It was. My use of computers was purely utilitarian. I have absolutely no interest in the theories behind how they work, or the details of what makes one model better than another. I just expect them to do what I need them to do, when I need them to do it, and try not to throw too much of a childish fit when they don't (at which I often don't succeed).

Penny rubbed the bridge of her aquiline nose. "I only learned about them in the first place because I needed to make a website to promote my band, then I got into recording and editing music electronically. My point is that this isn't really my specialty. I only know a few tricks I picked up from some friends and things I've read up on a little here and there. I'm not even close to being a real hacker, at best I just dabble."

I wasn't buying her sudden self pity, I knew she was underestimating herself. She was just temporarily burnt out. Penny often keeps too many balls up in the air and pushes herself too hard. She's always working on multiple projects at once, her mind is always racing, working on one problem or another. It shouldn't have been so shocking that she was crashing like this. It was inevitable. What was really shocking was that it didn't happen more frequently.

"You've always done great in the past when you've tackled something like this," I told her. "It sounds like you're already on the cusp of finding out something that might bust this case wide open. Don't give up. Take a break and come back to it when you're feeling more refreshed–that's an order!"

"Okay, you're the boss, boss. I'm just feeling irritated because I feel like if I knew some more about her, I could guess the right password before the software does. It might really speed things up. That's why I need to check out those notebooks." She explained.

I suppose I was hesitant because I already felt some guilt over violating Melissa's privacy by reading through her notebooks. This was bad enough, now I was about to let my assistant do it too? But what the hell, why not? Was letting her go through her notebooks really any better or worse than letting her go through her computer? It was a ridiculous double standard. Both things likely contained intimate thoughts that she didn't want exposed. If we ever met the poor girl, we'd know everything about her, maybe even more than her parents did - which would be a little awkward to say the least! Yet, we were professionals, and this was simply a routine part of our job - uncovering secrets to get to the truth. I had to do what I had to do, especially if it might bring her home safely.

"Okay, no problemo. I left 'em on my desk. Have at them if you really think they'll be of any help. Do you have anything else for me before I head out?"

Penny thought about it for a second before responding. "Yeah, what's her date of birth? People often use some variation of that in their passwords."

"It should be on one of the forms her parents filled out already." I was surprised Penny had forgotten that. She had clients fill out those forms all the time, and on top of that, she also scanned them into our computers. She was all too aware of the kind of information contained on our forms. It just went to show how fatigued she must've been feeling that such basic stuff was now slipping her mind.

"Oh duh! Yeah, that's right! I'll just look it up." She made a face, obviously feeling slightly embarrassed by her minor oversight. Her crestfallen expression made me feel the need to reassure her yet again.

"Don't sweat it, like I already said, you're doing a great job on this. I know you can do it. I'll see ya later." I hoped my words would boost her flagging confidence rather than add any additional pressure. From the new look on her face, it seemed to have had the desired effect.

"Yeah, thanks. Happy hunting." She wished me with her crooked smile.

I sincerely doubt there's going to be anything happy about the kind of hunting I'm about to do. I thought as I stepped out the door.

Once I got into Raritan I stopped by the home of the first girl I had permission to interview. Her name was Star, which is a pretty cool name in my opinion. I knew a girl back in my hometown of Barnegat, NJ with that same name, however it suited her much more than it did this Star who was not nearly as effervescent. This Star didn't shine so brightly, and the sparkle was missing from her eyes. She seemed downright sullen and dour. I shouldn't be so harsh of a judge of her character though, she was probably pretty upset about her missing friend, and her dad was hovering around during the entire interview, much to my chagrin. Hell, if I had to deal with this guy as my dad, I'd probably be a real Debbie downer too! As it turned out, he was a real piece of work.

I didn't like him being around since I was afraid that his presence would prevent her from opening up to me, also the dude was sort of rude. I'd set up the interview with the kid's mom, who had seemed quite congenial over the phone, but now she'd stepped out to go to the grocery store for something or other and I was left to fend for myself with this somewhat hostile guy lurking in the background.

I knew things weren't going to go well when he interrupted my questions to complain "I don't understand the point of all of this! The cops already stopped by here a few days ago and asked all the same kinds of questions."

This was news to me. It was something that hadn't appeared in the copy of the police report in my files. This was because what I had was the initial report from the same day Melissa had disappeared. Apparently, the cops were still putting some kind of effort into this case. Perhaps the daily searches Melissa's dad was conducting and all the flyers he was putting up all over town had put some pressure on them to take things a bit more seriously? In any case I considered it to be a positive development. The more people looking for her the better as far as I was concerned.

Her dad wasn't done with hassling me yet, unfortunately. "Are you even a real detective?"

"I'm fully licensed as a private investigator both here and in NY." I replied neutrally.

He snorted in derision. "So let me guess: you're an ex-cop who decided he could make more money charging people for his services, huh?" I wasn't sure what this guy's problem with me was exactly, but it was getting harder and harder for me to keep things civil every time he opened his mouth. I didn't want to give him the satisfaction of knowing that he was rattling my cage though, so I tried to play it cool. I've run afoul of this sort of attitude before, people who treated me like I was rent-a-cop and acted like I was a joke.

"No, actually. I was never a cop, but I was trained by one." I answered, resolving not to divulge any more personal details to this clown.

Max, my mentor, had been a member of the NYPD who'd been forced out when he took a stand against the corruption in his precinct. He'd opened a detective agency where I had worked while I was in college at Columbia University. Once I had enough experience under my belt, I opened my own small agency with his blessing. Randy had followed a similar path, working as an investigator while he was a student at Rutgers until he had enough years of experience under his belt to become fully licensed. The major difference being that I took him on as a partner in my own agency at that point.

I always felt like the fact that I had never been a cop, that I'd never been indoctrinated into that culture, gave me a certain advantage as an investigator. It helped me to look at things from a different perspective than how your average cop might. Sometimes it also created barriers too, not having ever been part of that fraternity. Yet it was worth it to me because that wasn't a club I felt I really wanted to be a part of. None of this was any of this prick's business though, so I kept my trap shut about it.

My last answer seemed to have satisfied him, or perhaps he just got bored with the game, because he left the room afterwards. I could now finish up my questions for Star without him hovering over us like an oppressive cloud. She didn't know anything of any real value to me.

It was yet another dead end, although her dad's unwarranted hostility made me wonder if I should consider him as a possible suspect? Why else be such a jerk when a little girl's safety was at stake? Especially one who was friends with your own daughter? I had to remind myself that this could all mean nothing. I tried to put myself in his shoes for a minute. Could it just be that he didn't like a stranger coming into his home and asking his kid a bunch of questions that she'd already given to the proper authorities? I guess I could understand that. Yet, I couldn't help but wonder if there was something more sinister at work here.

Perhaps he had developed an unnatural attraction to Melissa and acted upon it? If he was some kind of a pedophile, that could also explain his daughter's withdrawn demeanor–she could be a victim too. Now that he wasn't around, I tried to ask Star a few questions that might subtly hint at that, but once again, it didn't really lead me anywhere. This was a particularly nasty possibility that I couldn't completely dismiss, but I also didn't have anything solid to back it up other than a general dislike of the man, which certainly wasn't enough upon which to make such a serious accusation. Just because the guy got mouthy with me and his daughter was shy and a little spaced out it didn't mean that he was a pervert. Nevertheless, I decided to have Penny look into his background when I got back to the office.

By the time I'd finished up at Star's house, it was practically time for me to be at Erica's place, so I hurried over there. Fortunately, the two homes were only a few blocks away from each other, so I still arrived on time. I'm kind of a fan of punctuality, but I try not to be a dick about it.

The interview at Erica's house was far more productive. I was also pleased that the atmosphere at the house was 180 degrees different. Her parents were both extremely friendly and accommodating, eager to do whatever it took to help get Melissa safely back home. I realized that I had seen Erica's dad before. He had been part of the nightly search parties organized by Melissa's dad. Erica was quite chatty. She was Melissa's best friend and gave me lots of information that wasn't directly pertinent to the case but was still interesting. It helped me to reconstruct in my mind a more complete picture of what Melissa's world and her life was like. It appeared that in recent months the friends had been drifting apart somewhat. Melissa was spending less and less time with other people, and she was always online. When I asked if she knew what she was doing online, Erica suddenly got quiet and looked around, to make sure we were still alone.

"I haven't told anyone else this yet, not even the police. I don't want her to get into trouble." She said in an uncertain tone.

"I'd say she's already in trouble, wouldn't you? She might be in even bigger trouble if you know something and don't tell anyone." I said, then decided I was probably laying it on a little thick. In a softer voice I said "It's okay, I promise that I'll keep this between just the two of us. I only want to help her."

"Alright." She sighed, "She's been going into some chat rooms lately. She met a guy there that she really liked." As she said it her voice was quavering.

My heart sank into my stomach. I felt no elation, no joy that one of my biggest suspicions about this case from the very beginning might have some truth to it.

"I heard that she thought that most guys around her own age were too childish for her." I stated leadingly.

"Yeah, exactly. The boys at our school are all a bunch of jerks or idiots. That's why she started looking elsewhere."

I wasn't too surprised to discover that her best friend shared this attitude. They saw eye to eye on lots of things, apparently this was why they got along so well.

"Do you know the name of the websites she was on?"

"No, I really don't know much. I didn't really approve of what she was doing. I've heard about how that can go bad, so

I tried to talk her out of doing it, but she wouldn't listen. I mean, anyone could be in there pretending to be something that they're not. I kinda didn't want to know about it, I tuned her out whenever she tried to talk to me about it. Maybe I was even a little jealous too. This guy was starting to matter to her more than her real friends did."

"You must know something about this guy, though, right? She probably liked to talk about him if she was so into him." I insisted.

"Yeah, but I was only half listening. From what I can remember though, he was an older guy though, of course."

"Of course," I agreed conspiratorially. "How much older are we talking about? Not as old as me, right?"

"Don't be gross! No, he's a senior in some other high school. At least, that's what he told her."

"What High School did he say he went to?"

"Someplace I never heard of. Out in Minnesota I think."

"Minnesota!" I exclaimed.

She laughed a little. "Yeah, that's what I said too! I was like, what's the point of talking to someone who lives all the way out there? You're never gonna get to meet him–if that's even who he really is and not some sick loser living in his parent's basement."

Erica's face now took on a sad expression. "But she said she didn't care about all that. She just liked the way he made her feel. That he was the only person who really understands her. I couldn't stand to hear her talk like that, it made me feel so..." her voice trailed off, at a loss for the right words.

"Irrelevant?"

"Sure, that works. I got mad at her after that conversation. Like our friendship didn't matter to her anymore, so why should I even bother? I avoided her. She didn't even seem to notice, and now..." she started sobbing then tears gushed out of her eyes and ran down her cheeks, plopping into pools that formed on the kitchen table where we sat facing each other.

I awkwardly stretched out my hand and patted her shoulder.

"I never would've ignored her if I knew that she'd be gone!" She blurred out between crying fits.

"How could you have known? You can't blame yourself." It's so easy to say this sort of thing when you're not the one gripped by this kind of guilt. It seems so reasonable, so obvious when it isn't you.

Thankfully, she got herself back under control quickly. I was a little worried that her parents would get mad at me if they thought I was upsetting their daughter. I wondered how difficult it must've been for her to hold all of this guilt in for so long.

"Is that everything you know about this guy? Do you know his name?"

"It was Nick. I don't know the last name, if he ever gave her one."

"Do you think she ran away to be with this Nick guy?"

"I don't know. I don't see how she could get all the way out to Minnesota by herself. Even if she got there, how could they be together? He's supposed to still be in High School! His parents wouldn't let some random girl just move in with them. It doesn't make any sense!"

I had to admire her reasoning. She'd obviously given the situation a great deal of thought. She'd probably thought of little else for the past few days.

"But I don't know what she's been thinking lately. We barely spoke at all for the last few weeks." The guilt was back in her voice.

"Did she seem more upset than usual? Unhappy at home?"

"No, not any more than usual, but it's hard to say for sure."

I nodded. I could appreciate how such a thing would be difficult to gauge without talking to her as regularly as she once did.

I asked a few more questions to try and get a better sense of Melissa's home life. To see if she was generally unhappy at home or if there were any problems in the house I was unaware of that might make her want to leave. As far Erica could tell this wasn't the case, beyond Melissa just wanting a bit more attention from her parents sometimes.

I told her she had been a big help, because she had been, and thanked her for trusting me with the information she'd given me. While I'd been speaking to her, I'd gotten a call from the parents of Kathy, the last of Melissa's close friends. They said it was okay if I came by their house when I was done interviewing Erica.

So that is exactly what I did. Kathy's parents were as easy to get along with as Erica's had been, but Kathy had nothing useful for me in the way of new information. She was the most peripheral of Melissa's friends, although it sounded like lately she had nothing but friends circling the edges of her life ever since Nick had come into the picture.

This whole Nick situation filled me with dread, but I tried to tell myself that I could be reading too much into it. It really could be some teenager out in Minnesota, in which case it might just be another dead end. Then again, it could be the key to everything, especially if this person was even older and much closer than they claimed to be.

I tried not to let it worry me too much as I drove back to the office, instead I tried to rock out to whatever I could find on the radio, but 'try' is the operative word here. For whatever reason, I was unable to find anything that I was in the mood for. Every song seemed to annoy me, and I was constantly turning the dial until I gave up and turned it off. It was beginning to look like it was time to bite the bullet and invest in getting satellite radio.

When I got back into the office, Penny had an odd look on her face. It was like something halfway between joy and worry. She had a thick stack of papers next to her that she was reading through.

"Matt! I hacked into that other profile!" She said excitedly, setting down the paper she'd been looking at.

"Great! How did ya do it?"

"The notebooks gave me the name of her goldfish, and the password was the fish's name and Melissa's age." She said

"Great work! Find anything?"

"Oh yeah, you can say that again! She had a folder where she kept copies of all these conversations she had with some guy. I'm not even sure what website they were chatting on, she deleted her history religiously, but she copied and pasted lots of the conversations she had there. I guess they had some sentimental value to her."

"This guy's name wouldn't happen to be Nick, would it?"

"Yeah! How did you know?"

"One of her friends knew about it."

"Oh, that makes sense, it sounds like things were starting to get pretty serious between them."

I raised an eyebrow. "How serious?" I really didn't want to know, but I was obligated to.

"They considered each other to be married to one another." Penny said. I'd heard of this phenomenon before, people in long distance relationships on the internet pretending that they were in a state of virtual matrimony. It was just one more of the countless ridiculous things that lonely people sometimes do.

"That's not the worst part, though. Sometimes these conversations get a little steamy. I know I wouldn't be happy if I had a kid that was talking to anyone like that. I'd rip the goddamned computer out of their room!"

"Ugh. That bad, huh?"

"Yes. Thank God there's not too much of that, but it still shows up frequently enough to cause nausea. Maybe it gets more intense? I dunno, I haven't read through all of these yet." She tapped her long nails on the stack of papers.

"You printed them all out?" I asked superfluously.

"Yessir, all in chronological order for your viewing displeasure. I know how much you hate reading shit off of a screen."

"It's not good for your eyes! That's why I don't need any glasses yet!" I insisted.

"Hmm. I suspect it might be a little more complicated than that! Anyhow, feel free to take these with you and go through it all."

"Well, I guess now I know what I'll be reading tonight. Let's call it a day. Tomorrow I want you to see if you can figure out what site these messages came from. Also, I need you to run a background check on Star's dad."

"Really? You think he's a suspect? I'm thinking it's pretty obvious that she ran off with her hubby Nick."

"It's probably nothing. The guy just rubbed me the wrong way. But then again, for all we know, he could be Nick."

"Yuck!"

"Yeah, I know."

I scooped up the voluminous stack of papers to put them in my briefcase. I was *not* looking forward to having to go through these conversations. I could just leave it until tomorrow and do it at the office. It wasn't always such a good idea to bring my work home with me like this, and I'd already done so the night before. However, a kid's life might be at stake, so there was really no question that this is what I'd be doing with myself tonight.

At home I read through the transcript of Melissa and Nick's online conversations after dinner. I won't bore you with all the details, I'll just give my overall impressions. It starts out with some innocent getting to know you questions.

The early exchanges are a bit childish, but also kind of sweet and cute. It definitely reminded me of the sort of fluffy, meaningless content in the notes I used to pass to my girlfriends when I was that age.

Over time, the messages get more personal, mostly on Melissa's part. She's the one who shares the most personal information. Nick rarely talks much about himself, mostly he just offers her a shoulder to cry on, someone to confide in who is perpetually supportive. He's always got a positive platitude to offer, or automatic validation for her feelings. It's easy to see how easily someone could get addicted to that sort of instant emotional gratification. The fact that he rarely ever leans on her, that he doesn't talk much about his own troubles and needs was sticking out like a red flag to me. He seems too perfect, too supportive, almost inhumanly so. Like someone just playing the role of the perfect boyfriend rather than a real person. I could also see how she was too blinded by this so-called perfection to see it for what it really was.

As time wears on, things get more intense. They confess their love for one another. They make all kinds of pie in the sky kinds of plans for the future. I find out that Nick is (supposedly) a freshman in college. Being a high school Senior (which was bad enough) was a lie Melissa told. She also led him to believe that she was really 16, but even so, the age gap between them is too great at that age. Things sometimes get pretty inappropriate, there's some discussion about how experienced or inexperienced they are sexually and what sorts of things they'd like to try out or do to each other. That stuff was pretty unpleasant to read through considering her actual age. I couldn't help but notice that Nick was also the one who typically initiated that sort of talk. It was also becoming more frequent.

Near the end of the transcript, he talks about driving out to this area of the country during his spring break, allegedly under the pretense of visiting a sick uncle. They make plans to meet up once he's closer. The messages had time stamps on them, and the last exchange happened the same day that Melissa went missing. He was going to meet her in a park a few blocks away from her home at midnight.

This was the smoking gun I was looking for. The plan was for them just to meet up and maybe mess around a little, but she was supposed to return home, not run away with him. Even though this had all happened a few days ago, I decided to visit that park first thing in the morning to see if there were any clues still left behind there from their meeting. It was the last place where I knew she had probably been, so I had to check it out. Maybe I'd even have to bring Randy there to do one of his 'tracer' spells.

I also hoped that Penny would be able to figure out what website they'd been conversing on. Maybe she could work a little of her computer magic and figure out who was behind his profile? I feared that such things might be beyond her skill set. However, I could also tell that she was starting to get as obsessed with solving this case as I was. It was impossible to read Melissa's notebooks without feeling some kind of attachment to her. Perhaps her determination would help her to keep on working her miracles?

Things were moving beyond my own ability to properly resolve. I realized that I might soon have to turn all my information over to the police very soon, maybe even the FBI. If this guy was really from out of state this would now make this into a possible case of abducting a child over state lines which fell firmly under the Fed's jurisdiction. They would definitely have the resources to figure out who was really behind 'Nick's' online profile if Penny didn't get any results.

I was sick with worry over what might have really happened to Melissa. Her intention had only been to meet up with Nick, not run away. That was clear from both her own words and the fact that she didn't pack a bag. It was also clear to me that Nick wasn't who he claimed to be. A college kid living in a dorm as he described himself probably wouldn't have any place to hide Melissa if they had decided to run off together at the last minute. It was looking more and more like someone had lured her out to the park and abducted her. If kidnapping had been the goal, then where was the ransom note? I feared she'd been taken for some other sick end.

Once again, I'd lost track of time as I read over the transcripts. Naomi visited the home office where I'd isolated myself to remind me to come to bed. Tonight at least I'd managed to make it home in time for dinner, and I'd brought her up to speed on the case. However, I'd never mentioned that she'd put Randy up to offering his 'special' brand of help, nor had she (nor that I expected her to tip her hand like that). The whole matter had hung over the dinner like the proverbial elephant in the room. Now that we were alone together, without the kids around, I decided to finally address it.

"Randy spoke to me today about using his magic to help find Melissa." I said neutrally, studying her face as I said it.

"Oh really? Not a bad idea if I do say so myself." She couldn't help but smirk slyly as she said it.

"You can stop pretending. I know you put him up to it."

"Damn! That dude just can't keep a secret, can he?" She complained.

I smiled. "Neither of you can keep one from me, I know you both too well."

"You're not mad?"

"No, of course not," I assured her. "I know that you both mean well and it comes from a good place, a place of concern for both me and Melissa. Hell, I would've been disappointed in you if you'd given up on the idea so easily! Anyway, I'd definitely rather take Randy's help than go begging the ABC for it. I didn't know he could do a spell like the one he described to me, I can see how it could really come in handy. The way things are starting to look from what I've just read here, I might just have to take him up on his offer."

Naomi sighed in relief. "I'm happy to hear it! Maybe that thick skull of yours isn't quite so impenetrable after all?"

"But," I held up a finger, "I still wanna try things my way a little more first. I got a lot closer to solving this thing today using purely conventional means. I'm still not convinced I need to use the supernatural to crack this one–but I'm also not totally close minded to the idea anymore. Let me see how things go tomorrow, what other secrets Penny can pull out of her bag of tricks before I start calling in Mr. Wizard."

"Sounds fair enough. Now come to bed already! I've got a very special case of my own that I'd like you to investigate if ya know what I mean?" She winked at me with all the subtlety of a neon sign.

"Hmm, I suppose I could clear my schedule and look into it..." I teased.

"Buster, I need you to do a whole lot more than just look at it!" She laughed.

"Don't worry, I plan to fill all your needs!"

"Great! But you have to catch me first!" With that she ran out of the room and up the stairs.

I chased after her, up into our bedroom and before too long we were tearing each other's clothes off and making love like we were ten years younger. Hopefully the kids didn't hear us. Over the years we'd gotten pretty good at keeping things down, but it's hard to do when you start to get carried away, and that night I definitely let myself get carried away!

It was just what I needed to release some of the tension that had been building up inside of me ever since I'd taken on this case. Afterwards, we held each other's naked, sweat-slicked bodies close. I drifted off into a pleasant, euphoric sleep that was free of the nightmares that had plagued me the night before.

It was to be the last time I'd ever sleep so well ever again.

INVESTIGATION DAY THREE

When I got into the office the next morning, Penny was already there as usual. She looked like she'd never left.

"Please tell me that you haven't been here working on this all night." She was a notorious insomniac. Usually, she stayed up late working on her music, but sometimes the research I sometimes gave her to do consumed her attention instead.

"What? No! Of course not. I'm in a change of clothes aren't I? Where's your great observational skills?"

I was a little embarrassed that I hadn't noticed that now that she pointed it out.

"No, I didn't stay *here* all night. That would be silly. I brought this stuff home and worked on it there instead. It's much more comfortable there."

"Penny!" I admonished her, but I was also secretly proud of her devotion to the cause.

"Before you lecture me again on maintaining healthy boundaries between home and work, which is something you fail to do all the time, I might add, do you at least want to hear what I've found out?"

I did. "Okay, spill it. It had better be good."

"I don't know if I'd call it 'good" but it *is* progress."

"Shit! Don't keep me in suspense!"

"Not only did I figure out what website they were talking on, but I found out that Nick is still active on it. So I made a profile for myself and started talking to him last night."

"You what?" I was aghast. "Why? Don't you know how dangerous that is?"

"I thought maybe we could set a trap for him. I could set up a meeting with him somewhere, but when I don't show up, you tail him back to his place. Maybe the creep is holding Melissa there."

Honestly, it was a pretty good plan, but I wasn't comfortable with her flirting with him like this. "So he really seems interested in you?"

"Oh yeah. The guy is a total creep. All that talk about how much he loves Melissa in her chats with him, but the minute I show up and start talking to him he's all over me. I figured he must be into the young stuff, so I told him I was fifteen and sent him some phony pictures I found online. He sent back some equally fake ones."

"Jesus!" I swore, still not sure what to do with this new information. "So you're thinking that he's actually local then?"

"Oh yeah! Uncomfortably so! I hacked his IP address and I was able to trace the computer he was talking to me on to within a few miles of its actual location. It looks like it's somewhere in Highland Park."

This astounded me. My office is located in New Brunswick, NJ and Highland Park is literally the next town over. I was equally impressed with Penny's hacking skills.

"That close huh?"

"Spooky isn't it?"

"Well, great job with the computer stuff. See, you're a good hacker after all."

"I can't claim all the credit, I did have to call a friend." She confessed.

"It doesn't matter, you got the job done! Is he still on there now?" I asked, pointing to Penny's personal laptop, which was on the desk next to Melissa's computer.

"Nah. He said our goodbyes a few hours ago."

"We'll try to keep him on the hook, see what information you can get out of him about himself, although most of it is probably bullshit, there's often a few grains of truth in every lie. See if he'll agree to meeting you somewhere nearby."

"Roger that," She pursed her lips and looked at me expectantly. "So what's your plan of attack for today?"

"Nick was supposed to meet Melissa at a park near her house the same night she disappeared. I thought I might head over there and check it out. I just wanted to stop by here first, see if you'd found anything new and grab some coffee."

"If that park is the last place she was at, Randy could pick up the trail from there with his magic. Do you want me to send him to meet you there when he comes in?"

I thought about it. As much as I hated to use magic, it made the most sense at this point. I wasn't all that likely to find anything at the park that would lead me right to her without it. Penny had narrowed 'Nick's' location to Highland Park, but I still didn't know exactly where he was in that town or even what he looked like. Her plan to bait him was a good one, but it might take some time for him to agree to meet with her. The logic of it all was inescapable.

This would mean that I'd have to leave the Orb of Sinister inside the safe in my office, otherwise Randy wouldn't be able to work his spell at the park. The idea of doing so, with only Penny to guard it (she did have a pistol hidden in the top drawer of her desk and she was a decent shot with it) made me feel a little uneasy, but it had to be that way. It wasn't the first time I'd had to make this sort of a compromise. I would still bring the *Vermilion Avenger* with me, there was no point in leaving it behind since Penny wasn't trained in how to use it.

"Okay, yeah. I'll wait for him there. The place is called Frelinghuysen Park." I informed her. Then I recalled something.

"Hey, have you done that background check on Star's dad yet?"

"Yup. Nothing much there. He's squeaky clean, just has a few speeding tickets. Here's a copy." She handed me a printout, and I gave it a cursory look over. The fact that the guy didn't have a criminal record didn't mean anything, just that he was smart or lucky enough to avoid getting caught doing anything worse than having a lead foot. However, it was equally true that I was letting my own prejudices against the man color my perceptions. More than likely, this was another dead end.

I grabbed my coffee, this time pouring it into a thermos I kept for when I would be drinking it in my car, said my goodbyes to Penny and then I was off to Frelinghuysen Park. I wasn't sure what I was expecting to find there after an entire week had passed by, yet I felt drawn to the place as if by some unseen magnetic force. Randy was all about trusting your instincts and letting them guide you. Right now, my instincts were bringing me to this park.

Frelinghuysen Park seemed pleasant enough in the early morning light. It was a wide open area with a fenced off tennis court, a couple of baseball diamonds and a pool which was closed at this time of the year. There was also a basketball court and some playground equipment that I could see from where I was parked. I got out of my car, still holding my thermos in one hand, from which I would occasionally take a rejuvenating sip. The place was deserted at this time of day. The kids were in school and most adults were at work. My attention, for whatever reason, was drawn to a line of trees that bordered one end of the park. I started slowly walking towards it. As I passed the playground equipment, I thought about buying a slide and some swings for my daughter to play with in our backyard before she got too old to appreciate such things. Even though she was only four years old, she was already taking after her brother too much in that she spent most of her time inside playing video games instead of running around outside like I felt she should be doing.

I reached the trees, which was not a particularly thick grouping of them. It was still early Spring, and the leaves were just starting to come back on their branches. I walked parallel to the tree line scanning the ground ahead of me, not sure what I was really looking for. I tried to put myself in Melissa's shoes, imagining this place at night, her heart beating in anticipation at the idea of finally meeting someone that she'd only spoken with online. I didn't know where in the park they were supposed to find each other. I looked up and slowly turned my head around, taking in the panorama of the place when suddenly my foot kicked something on the ground in front of me.

I faced the ground again to see what it was that my foot had struck. What I saw next will haunt me forever. It's the worst thing I've ever seen in my life. It was a hand, a tiny, delicate hand. Connected to the hand was a body, stretched out on the ground near the trees. It was Melissa's body. She was fully dressed, but I could see cuts and bruises wherever her skin was exposed. Her hair was flipped up on one side to reveal that she was missing an ear. Her empty, lifeless eyes looked up at me like glassy orbs making an insensate accusation.

I twisted my head to the side and threw up before I had even consciously registered what I was doing. My mind reeled. She couldn't have been here all this time. Her body wasn't well concealed, so someone would've found it, and there was no smell to it. This all told me that she had been recently killed and the body dumped here, probably in the past few hours. I held onto these threads of logic like they were a lifeline, trying mightily to avoid thinking about how this grisly discovery actually made me *feel*. That was something I couldn't confront. I dare not. Because then I'd have to deal with what a failure I was because I hadn't been able to prevent this. With how I was to blame for it because my pride had prevented me from using all the resources at my command to find her sooner.

As I wiped the vomit from my lips with the back of my hairy hand, I realized that I was sobbing. Actually, blubbering might be a better word for it. My vision swam and the world was distorted by my tears as I swayed on my feet. I had to steady myself against a nearby tree trunk. I stood like that for several minutes, breathing heavily and crying my eyeballs out. Trying hard to think of nothing, to just empty my mind of all the guilt that was overwhelming it so that I could function long enough to do what must be done next. I had to call this in and report it to the local police. As I dug in my pocket for my cell phone, I was shocked to realize that my thermos was gone. I looked around wildly and saw that I'd dropped it in the grass near where Melissa's outstretched hand lay. Coffee trickled out of it, gushing towards her cold, gray fingers.

Great, I've contaminated the crime scene! I thought, as if this was the worst thing about the whole situation. I couldn't believe she was gone. This bright, talented kid who I was beginning to feel like I knew from her writings. What kind of a monster could do such a thing? And it was all my fault, I was certain of that. I could've stopped all this from happening if I hadn't wasted so much time uselessly dithering around.

Stop it! Get a grip! Call this in. I told myself as I lifted the phone out of my pocket with a trembling hand and dialed 911. I tried not to look at the horrible sight of the body only a few feet away from me as I lifted the phone to my face.

Anger surged through my body. Anger at myself, anger at the killer, anger at this whole rotten world where such things were possible.

It wasn't long before the entire park was swarming with police and paramedics. They had plenty of questions for me, and I explained how my own investigation had led me to the park. Now that this was a murder investigation, they wanted me to hand over Melissa's notebooks and computer to them. It was hoped that they could use Nick's IP address to lead them right to his door, since they had ways of dramatically narrowing down the area where his computer was. I readily agreed to hand over everything I had to them. They told me they'd stop by my office to retrieve the materials later on that day. I overheard one of the cops remark how the missing ear and the other marks on her body reminded him of a case he'd heard about from a cop in New Brunswick about how a prostitute's body had been found in similar condition a few months earlier. The comment sent a chill down my spine—were we dealing with a serial killer here?

Did I say that Melissa's body was the worst thing I'd ever seen? That's not quite true. When her parents showed up at the park before the body was removed, drawn by all the activity happening down the street–that was the worst thing I'd ever seen. It was all too easy to place myself in their shoes. I couldn't imagine what it must be like to see your own child like that. I prayed I never would. It was terrible to watch all hope fade from their eyes as they collapsed into a screaming, sobbing heap. Right then and there I decided I wouldn't be charging them for this investigation. I certainly didn't need the money, and I would've felt like a scumbag charging them after how I had failed them.

Randy showed up in the middle of this circus. The cops were done talking to me (for now), so I made my way over to where I saw him standing on the edge of the crowd that had gathered on the other side of the crime scene tape. I quickly explained what was going on. Randy was at a loss for words at first, then he looked at me curiously.

"How are you holding up, Matt? Are you going to be okay? Your aura is a mess right now."

"I'll get through it." I lied. "Come over to my car, I have one of Melissa's notebooks in my briefcase, I thought you could use it to do that spell before I have to give it to the police."

He blinked at me in confusion from behind his thick glasses.

"What good will that do? The spell leads me to her–and she's right over there."

"There's gotta be something we can still do to help nail this dirtbag!"

"What do you mean, nail him? Shouldn't we leave this to the proper authorities now?"

"I thought if we could figure out where he took her, we could give that information to the police." I was lying again. If I found out where this person was living, I fully intended to kill him myself. I had the *Vermilion Avenger* with me that day and I intended to put it to good use. I felt like I owed it to Melissa and her family. I had arrived too late to save her, but at least I could make sure that the sort of person that was capable of this atrocity wouldn't live to do it to anyone else ever again. Perhaps in his execution I could find some chance of redemption for myself from my own culpability in this crime?

"It's the least I can do after I fucked this up so badly. If only I hadn't been so stubborn, if only I'd listened to you and Naomi..."

"This isn't your fault man, you can't blame yourself!" He tried to reassure me, but I wasn't having any of it.

"Isn't it though? Look, are you gonna help me out or what?"

Randy looked thoughtful for a minute. "I think there might be a way to modify the spell so that it will show me the path she took from this park the last time she was here when she was still... alive."

"Do it!" I urged him. I wasn't too surprised by this. From what I understood Randy was, even at his young age, considered to be a great wizard partiality because he was so good at improvising improvements to existing spells.

"Okay, show me that notebook and I'll see what I can do."

I led him back to where I was parked. I took the notebook from my briefcase and handed it over to him.

"I'm gonna work on this in my car and if I get any results, I'll call you on your cell. Wait for me, this might take a few minutes." He told me as he took the notebook in his hand.

I spent a few tense minutes just sitting there in my car, watching the crime scene as it was processed and fighting back another wave of tears. So many feelings raced through my mind. Self pity and hatred over my inability to prevent this horror from unfolding, sympathy for Melissa's family, but chief amongst all these emotions was a burning, white hot anger at the monster who was responsible. I longed to make him pay. It was the only way I could restore some semblance of sanity to my world, because I didn't want to live in a world where someone could do something like this without any kind of consequences.

I was old enough to already know that life was often too brief, cruel and unfair. But like the rest of us, I didn't spend all my time concentrating on that. I lost myself in silly distractions and tried instead to concentrate on the more delightful aspects of our existence. It was a hell of a thing to be slapped in the face like this. To be woken up from the pleasant dream world we delude ourselves into thinking we inhabit and to have the full ugliness of life shoved right into your face like that. Our sense of security is nothing but an illusion, a lie. The most precious things in our lives can be ripped away and hollowed out in the blink of an eye.

This life is a kind of hell. A hell where bright, beautiful kids with endless talent and potential can be reduced to being nothing but a plaything for some madman's amusement, then discarded like trash once they lose interest in the game. How do you run and hide away from that dark reality? How can you deny it when it's right in front of you for all to see? I couldn't turn back time, but I could still try to find some way to balance the scales, to make it right. I desperately needed to believe in something true. I needed to know that justice could be real and not just some unattainable abstraction. I would make it so or die trying.

I couldn't give up now.

My phone vibrated on my dashboard, snapping me back to the present. Randy's voice came to me from the other end. "'Matt, I've done it! I can see a path going down the road, get ready to follow behind me, I'm about to pull out of this parking lot and see where it goes."

"Great work, kid! I'll be right behind you." I couldn't see jack shit, but I didn't expect to. I understood enough about this kind of magic to know that only the spellcaster could see the path that Randy had conjured up.

As I trailed behind Randy's car, a beat up, old white early 90's Hyundai Excel that I had once owned, I started to become increasingly confused. The roads we were taking weren't leading us in the direction I'd expected that they would–in towards Highland Park. Instead, we were heading farther north. This had to be some mistake? Yet Randy was far from being the tired old trope of the bumbling magician, he knew what he was doing, if nothing else I had faith in that. Perhaps the killer had some other location that he took his victims to? It wasn't unheard of. If so, he might not be there right now, but I could set up surveillance around the place, then ambush him when he returned. I could even possibly get his home address by researching who owned the place.

Suddenly, Randy pulled over to the side of the road. Wondering what was up, I followed suit and pulled in behind him. I climbed out of my car and walked over to his door. He already had the window pulled down by the time I got there.

"What's up? Why'd we stop?" I demanded, trying to sound milder about it than I really felt. I hated to be interrupted like this. My heart had been pounding at the thrill of the chase, my mind swimming with dark fantasies about the things I'd do to the killer once I found him.

"The trail's gone. It ended a few feet back."

"What do you mean it's gone? It didn't lead anywhere!"

"I told you, these spells only have a range of a few miles. Once you get beyond that range, the path just ends–whether you've reached the end or not."

I cursed loudly and banged a fist on top of his car. I did recall him mentioning this before now that I thought about it.

"Can't you change the spell again? Make the range longer?" I asked in desperation.

"I've already done that. There's no more extending it. It's just not possible."

I cursed again, but this time I spared Randy's car and my hand, which was now throbbing with pain from my last overly emotional outburst. Instead, I ran it through my hair.

"Okay, okay. How about this? Why don't you try to summon Melissa's spirit? Maybe we could just ask her if she knows who killed her?" I knew that such things were possible. I'd been forced to solve a case by cheating like this once before.

Randy looked at me skeptically. "I don't think that her spirit is still here on this plane. Otherwise, I think I would've sensed her presence at the crime scene. I'm pretty sure that she's already moved on."

"*Pretty sure?*" I replied mockingly. "That's not good enough! We're after a killer here, maybe even a serial killer! Can you be more definite than that?"

Randy sighed. "Okay. I'll try to reach out to her, but it won't be easy. It's not Halloween or El Día De Los Muertos like it was the last time we tried something like that. The walls between the worlds are much thicker right now."

Randy took up Melissa's notebook from the passenger seat next to him and put himself into a kind of a trance by chanting magic words in an obscure ancient language that Naomi calls *M'bogish* which predates even Indo European. I won't go into any more details than that. If anyone should ever read this account, I don't want them trying to duplicate Randy's spells, as it can be extremely dangerous for an amateur to mess around with this sort of stuff.

Suffice it to say that after several minutes, Randy came out of his trance and looked at me sadly. "I'm certain that she's gone. She's somewhere in the Aether now."

The Aether was a universe of psychic energy where the hopes, dreams, and nightmares of humanity's collective consciousness take on a reality of their own. There were many different "Afterlife Realms" there based upon all the different religious beliefs people held. It was to one of these realms where most people's souls went when they died. I knew–I'd been there once. I hadn't died, but it was possible for a living person to visit such a place if they knew how to astrally project, which is sort of the same thing as having an out of body experience. Randy had once taught me how to do this particular trick and guided me into the Aether–but that's another story for another time.

Knowing that death was not the end of our existence would probably be a comfort to most people, but it wasn't to me. The truth about the Aether wasn't particularly appealing to me, it was full of so-called Gods and demons that sucked up the adulation or terror of the souls that inhabit the place like a bunch of psychic vampires. Sometimes, it's better not to know the reality behind certain things so you can just keep on believing in all the happy fairy tales that we tell ourselves. Ignorance really is bliss.

I wasn't about to let the revelation that Melissa's soul was in the Aether blunt my determination to catch her murderer. "So what? Maybe we can find her there?"

"You know that looking for an individual soul over there is like looking for a needle in a haystack! We'll only get ourselves in trouble if we try. Besides, if she's found some peace over there I think we should just leave her be, it's the respectful thing to do."

"Peace? Over there?" I scoffed.

"Just because Heaven isn't your cup of tea, doesn't mean that other souls can't find happiness there. It's not for us to judge. I'm *not* going to open a portal to the Aether for us." He said it all with an uncharacteristic gravitas in his voice that told me this was not up for debate.

So that was that then. Although I could astrally project without Randy's help, I couldn't get into the Aether unless he did a spell that opened up a portal to it first.

I thanked Randy for all he had done so far and told him to just go back to working on the cases I'd put him on before I had him meet me at the park.

"Are you sure you're gonna be okay?" He asked. From the way he was eyeing me I could tell that he was studying my aura again. Internally, I raged against my inability to hide anything from him. He probably read that in my aura too, damn him!

"Honestly, I don't know. I'm gonna have to be, I guess. Not much of a choice, really." I said as I stared off vacantly into the clear blue sky on the other side of the road.

"There's always a choice. Just don't go off doing anything crazy, okay? This case is over and everything is out of our hands now. You've gotta let this go. I'm sorry that it ended like this, really I am. The important thing to remember is that none of this is your fault." The way he was talking to me you'd think that I was the junior partner and he was the boss!

"Yeah. I suppose you're right. I'll see you later, alright?" I lied to him again. It was starting to become a habit.

"Okay, take care, please." Concern was etched into his eyes as he said it. I nodded and he handed me back Melissa's notebook.

I returned to my car and just sat there for some time, long after Randy had driven off. I was numb to the world. I kept on looking out the window not really seeing anything that was there. I always carry a 9mm pistol on me in a hidden holster. I took it out and just let it sit there in my hand, feeling the weight of it dragging me down.

I've never confessed this to anyone before. Not even the counselor that the Guilds set me up with who suggested I write down this whole story. I guess I've been too ashamed to admit to it. Ashamed at my own selfish foolishness. I picked up that gun and put it in my mouth, letting the barrel sit on my tongue, feeling the cold, metallic tang of it. Melissa Hollins was dead because of me, and I wasn't sure I could live with that anymore.

Sure, the result would've been the same if her family had hired any other PI, but they hadn't. They hired me, and as much as I liked to pretend otherwise, I wasn't a normal PI anymore, I hadn't been for years now. There were things I and my friends could do that were beyond belief. But because I was afraid to embrace that weirdness, because I was so determined to hang onto a semblance of normalcy for my own comfort, a little girl was now dead. I had her blood on my hands as surely as if I'd killed her myself. I had killed her with my negligence, with my arrogance. I had never felt so useless before. What was the point of being a PI if I couldn't help save someone like Melissa? What was the point of me at all?

I don't know how long I sat there in my car on the side of the road with that gun shoved halfway down my throat. It could've been minutes or an hour. In the end, I took it out– obviously. I wish I could say that it was because I knew how much blowing my brains out would hurt my family. How I'd be robbing my kids of their father. How much it would hurt Naomi, whose life had already been shattered once already when she lost her own father at an early age, a loss which she'd spent most of her life trying to deal with. What would it do to her now to lose her own husband in such a terrible way? All of these things *did* cross my mind at some point or another as I struggled with the dilemma of whether or not to pull the trigger, but in the end, I don't think any of these reasons were what stopped me from giving in to the urge to do it. I think what really stopped me was the knowledge that what I really desired was complete oblivion. A complete cessation of all existence. Peace in nothingness.

It was something I knew wasn't possible. I'd already been beyond the veil of death once before and I knew that what awaited me there was just a different kind of universe, not the complete escape from the misery of my own thoughts that I so badly longed for. This act would do no good to anyone. I wouldn't be any closer to sweet oblivion and my family would be irrevocably shattered in the process.

Worse yet, Melissa's killer would still be out there, free to hurt more people. I couldn't stop him if the contents of my skull were splattered all over my windshield. But there was still a chance that I could get him. I remembered the trap I'd ordered Penny to set for him. It was a long shot, but it could work. I needed it to work. I wasn't content to let the police handle this. What if they screwed it up and he got away? Or they nabbed him, but the system let him walk? It wasn't just that. I realized that I *wanted* to kill him. It *had* to be me. Nothing else would come close to making me feel that any kind of real justice had been done. I *needed* this–as much for myself as for Melissa.

Remember how I said I didn't believe in moral absolutes? How I thought that everything was just a spectrum of different shades of grays? That there was no such thing as real evil, just lots of sick, sad, incredibly lost people making stupid desperate choices? It was now impossible to keep any holding faith in that idea as images of Melissa's ravaged corpse kept floating back up to the surface of my mind's eye.

This was true evil, of that there could be no doubt. Yes, evil was something real alright. What else could you call someone that could do such a thing to another human being?

This flawed notion of mine that evil wasn't real was partially influenced by the incredibly strange fact that I had once met the being that most people would call the Devil the last time I had been in the Aether, and surprisingly he really wasn't that bad at all. In fact, he was quite helpful. I've met lots of people who were much worse. Well, the Devil himself might just be nothing more than a scapegoat for the evils that mankind inflicts upon one another, but the idea he represents sure is real enough, and it lives inside of some of us. Hell let's be honest, there's probably more than enough of it in all of us, if you scratch below the surface deeply enough. This was the sobering reality that I had just awakened to, that I had for so long sought to deny. If evil was real, then it had to be eradicated in order for us (mostly) good people to be able to thrive. I had just nominated myself as the person who would take this burden on in this specific case at least. It was the only meaning I could find for myself in the face of all this senselessness.

Me, me, me. It was really all about me. Killing myself seemed so selfish, but so was staying alive for revenge. I can see now, with the clarity of hindsight that what this was really about was my own feelings of powerlessness. Failing to save Melissa made me feel ineffectual, incompetent and pointless. Being the one to guarantee that her killer got what he deserved might do the opposite for me. It was never about getting justice for Melissa so much as it was about trying to reclaim my own personal power and self-respect.

But I couldn't see any of that at that moment. I'd convinced myself that killing Melissa's killer would somehow fix everything. That I was doing it all for her. As if she'd even know. She was beyond such petty concerns now. I should've known that, but I refused to see it. I had given myself a new purpose, a new mission in life. Before, I'd been too spooked by the fantastic power at my command and an innocent girl had paid the ultimate price for my hubris. Now, I would make *sure* I used this power to its full extent to exact vengeance for her.

I put my gun back in its holster and drove back to my office. It was time to see if Penny's efforts had yet to yield any fruits.

I returned to the office with my briefcase in one hand and the case for the *Vermilion Avenger* in the other. I set them both down in a relatively free area on Penny's desk temporarily as I often did. As they thudded down she looked up at me with an unmistakable expression of pity on her face.

"You already know?" I asked uselessly.

"Randy called me and gave me a heads up. He said you were pretty upset about it. I can only imagine what it must've been like to be the one to find her like that, I'm so sorry Matt."

I must've been wearing an angry expression. She misinterpreted it as being angry over Randy filling her in, but I didn't mind that. Randy and Penny were forever dating each other off and on so frequently that nobody bothered to keep track of it anymore. Even when they weren't an item romantically, they always managed to get along like a house on fire. They were always as thick as thieves together and kept no secrets from one another. It would've been strange if Randy *hadn't* told her anything yet. If I looked angry it was likely because I hated being the object of anyone's pity. Or maybe it was any number of a million other stressors from that awful morning?

"Don't be mad about him telling me. Even if he hadn't said anything, I'd know. It's all over the local news now." She pointed to the TV that was hanging on the wall in the waiting room of the office opposite her desk. It was on mute, with the closed captioning on. I could see that the media had descended upon the park like the flock of vultures that they were. They must've arrived just after I'd left. Melissa's story was finally headline news. All she had to do was die to get their attention. I nodded numbly at the TV.

"Please turn that shit off." I ordered. Penny obediently scooped up the remote control next to her and cut it off completely.

"The silver lining is that I succeeded in getting Nick back into a chat with me. I still have him here online with me now. He's pretty eager to meet up with me soon, too. Not that it matters much now if we're just gonna hand over this whole thing to the police."

I did a double take. "What?" This was more than I could've hoped for. "See if you can meet with him tonight. Maybe… in the North Brunswick Walmart parking lot around nine."

Penny looked baffled by this request. "Why? Are we setting up a sting for the police?"

"Err, yeah. Something like that." I bluffed poorly. She shot me a quizzically arched eyebrow, then turned to her laptop.

She was obviously feeling some misgivings, but she was so accustomed to following my orders that her fingers now flew across her keyboard anyway. It was odd to contemplate that she was now in the midst of communicating with someone who was very likely a murderer.

"It's funny, but when we tried to follow Melissa's trail from the park, it didn't lead us in the direction of Highland Park." I mentioned as she typed.

Without looking up she replied. "There's a possibility that his computer isn't in that area at all. He could've been using a VPN to mask his true IP address."

I nodded even though I had no idea what a VPN was. Hell, I'm not even sure that I really even fully understood what an IP address was back then either. As the years have progressed though, I've been forced to become a bit more tech savvy to remain competitive in this industry, which has increasingly become dependent on computer literacy and using all kinds of gadgets.

"That's why it's important to lure him into a meeting. So I can trail him and give his real location to the cops." I was really getting good at lying to my best friends.

"That's probably not necessary, they have ways of getting his real IP and even pinpointing the location of his computer." She answered.

"Oh yeah? How long will that take them? This scumbag needs to be taken down *now* before he can hurt someone else! This can't wait, he's too dangerous! He's got no self-control! This guy just got done with Melissa and he's already trolling for his next victim by talking to you! The guy's gotta be a total serial killer! One of the cops even said that something he...did to her body looked just like another body that was found around here not too long ago."

Penny finally looked up from her screen and met my eyes. "Really? Damn! They're keeping all of that out of the news reports I've seen so far. They must not want to start a panic."

"Yeah, well it's true." I affirmed, like I was Moses carrying the commandments down from the mountain.

She whistled at the gravity of the situation and started typing again. A few more minutes passed, then the constant clicking and clacking of her nails on the keys abruptly ceased. She breathed out heavily and looked up at me again.

"It's done. He agreed. He actually agreed to meet with me tonight! He even gave me a description of his car and what part of the parking lot he plans to park in so I can find him more easily. Dude claims to drive a black Lexus, can you believe that? Doing pretty well for a first-year college student, huh?"

"Yeah, well I'm sure that whole bit about him being a student is just one more of the many lies he's telling about himself. Great work, by the way!"

"Thanks! Yeah, those cops'll really owe us one when they catch this creep, won't they? We did most of the work for them, didn't we? How much do you wanna bet we won't get any credit for catching him? Typical!" Penny said with a touch of pride in her voice. I wished I could feel the same sort of satisfaction, but I still felt like all I'd done was fail Melissa.

The last thing I was worried about was getting any kind of credit for my role in this fiasco.

"Hey, one more thing–the cops will be stopping by here later on to get Melissa's computer and notebooks. Do me a favor though, don't mention anything to them about setting up this meeting with Nick, at least not quite yet."

"What? Why?"

"They might not approve. I don't want to let them in on this until I've successfully trailed him back to his house."

She looked at me for a good, long minute. Then her eyes narrowed. "What's really going on here?" Suddenly she gasped.

"Omigod! Tell me you're not planning on killing him yourself or anything like that?"

I paused for probably too long before responding, betrayed by my lack of an effective poker face. "What? Where'd you get a crazy idea like that from? Is that what Randy told you? Does he really suspect I'm planning something like that? Is that what he thought he saw in my aura?" I tried to sound as offended as possible. Unfortunately, even though I did a little theater in High School, I never was much of an actor.

"Holy shit! I'm right, aren't I? You're really planning on doing it!" Her eyes were as wide as saucers now. Her voice was thick with disbelief and a note of something else.

Something that I wouldn't understand until later on. It was *horror*. She was either horrified by what I was planning or horrified by me. Probably both.

"I don't know what you're talking about! This is nuts!" I continued to protest uselessly.

"Matt, I've been doing this long enough to be able to see right through your bullshit. I don't need Randy to tell me what's on your mind. All he said was that you were really upset that Melissa's gone and you're blaming yourself."

I finally got tired of all the lies, all the pretending. "Yeah, well maybe you really don't know me as well as you think? I've killed plenty of people before, you know! And I can do it again if I have to." I said coldly. This was true, I had seen my fair share of gun fights since the Guilds came into my life. It wasn't something I was normally proud of or comfortable talking about. Real violence is very different from what you see in the movies, it's so much uglier and being a party to it makes you feel tainted. In the past, I'd always avoided killing whenever possible. I'd even figured out a way to use the hilt of the *Vermilion Avenger* like a club to knock people out with it instead of slicing them up with the business end.

"I know," She looked down. "But all those other times were different. That was all in self-defense. But this...you're making a plan to deliberately hunt down and murder someone. Can't you see how fucked up that is?"

"Not murder. Execution." I clarified.

"Call it whatever you want, but it's still wrong!" She insisted.

"Is it? I'd be making sure that a monster like that will never be able to hurt anyone ever again. I'd be doing a public service!"

She just shook her head sadly at me. I couldn't believe her hypocrisy! Penny had a mean streak too sometimes; I had seen it plenty of times in the past. The woman had a rotten, volcanic temper and a surprisingly vicious side that came out when she was outraged enough. Why couldn't she understand why this needed to be done?

"Don't act so high and mighty! You can't judge me! You weren't there! You didn't see what he did to her! I've seen how pissed off you get sometimes when you watch the news! I've heard you wish that certain people were dead too!"

"That's completely different and you know it! We all say some stupid shit like that in the heat of the moment that we don't really mean. I could never kill anyone in cold blood like you're planning on doing."

"But don't you at least want to see this guy get what's coming to him? I thought you were starting to get attached to Melissa too from reading through all of her stuff? Jesus Christ! If this guy has his way, *you'd* be his next victim!"

"Yes, I was really starting to care about her, too. She reminded me so much of myself at that age. Why do you think I stayed up half the night working on this case? I also want to see her get justice–but that's not what this is! I just can't believe you're really thinking about doing something like this! It's not like you at all!"

"Just stay out of it then. Let me do what I've gotta do. This doesn't concern you anymore!"

She shot straight up in her seat and stared me down. "Doesn't concern me? It doesn't concern me if someone who's my boss, and also one of my best friends gets himself locked up for murder? Someone whose kids genuinely think I'm their aunt? We're family Matt, maybe not by blood, but by choice. I know you're hurting right now, I know you think you could've done something to prevent all of this, but that's a bunch of bullshit too. You did everything you could do to try and help her, we all did. Sometimes it's just not enough. Sometimes no matter how hard we try, we can't bring about a happy ending. You can't change the past. Doing this won't bring Melissa back, it's just going to wreck your own life! Don't throw your life away over a piece of shit like Nick, he's not worth it! Don't let yourself become one of his victims too! " her eyes pleaded with me.

"I won't get locked up. The Guilds won't let that happen. I'm the Guardian of the Orb. I'm too valuable to them.They'll cover up my role in all of this if I ask them too. They've covered up worse things that their people have done."

She shook her head. "That might be true. But I won't be– *can't* be a part of it. I just set this whole thing up! Don't you understand? That makes me into an accessory to murder! Even if I never get prosecuted for it–*I would know.* I don't want to have to live with that on my conscience! If you were in your right mind you wouldn't expect me to either. You wouldn't have used me like that if you were thinking straight. If you're not going to call this off, then I'm going to have to resign."

I was floored by what she just said. Surely, she couldn't be serious? Penny was one of my most loyal friends.

"Excuse me?"

"You heard me! Give this idea up right now or I quit!"

"Fine! Quit then! I don't need you!"

She looked at me with an unimaginably hurt expression, full of sadness and disbelief. I've never seen her look so upset, either before or after this moment. It hurts my heart to look back on this argument, to relive seeing that terrible look on her face and to know that I was the one who put it there.

"So that's it, huh? Your obsession with getting revenge on behalf of someone who you've never even really met is worth more to you than eight years of loyal friendship? I thought I meant something to you, I thought we were family, but I guess I was wrong. Maybe you're right? Maybe I don't know you after all? Maybe I never really did? I didn't think you were capable of something like this. I believed in you. I thought you were better than this, but it turns out that you're just another asshole, Matt Spike, and I quit!" She was crying now, her thick mascara running down her cheeks as she angrily began gathering up her things from the desk and tossing them into the backpack she carried her stuff around in back then.

As she closed up her laptop and shoved it into her bag, I was struck by a new fear. "Don't try to stop me, Penny. Don't say anything to the cops. Don't try to warn Nick that I'm coming for him. Just let things play out the way that they have to. This is the best way to make sure he'll never kill again. Deep down somewhere inside yourself know that it's true. You know that this is right. You know that we can't trust the police or the system not to fuck this one up. He's not a human being anymore, he's like a sick animal that needs to be culled from the herd before he does any more damage. I need to make sure that he dies for what he's done. For what he did to a helpless, innocent *child!* What if it had been my daughter? It could be someday if I don't act now! Nobody else should have to suffer again like Melissa's parents are right now. Please, just let me do this one thing, and then once it's over everything can go back to normal again."

She zipped up her bag and looked into my eyes again challengingly. "And what if I did say something, Matt? How are you going to stop me? Are you going to hurt me too?"

Just then, the *Vermilion Avenger* burst out of the case that it constantly hovered inside of, breaking the locks. It happened so quickly that I could barely register what was happening but thank goodness I did. I shouted in surprise and managed to reach out with my mind and stop the massive sword just in the nick of time. It had stopped mere inches from her face. It hung there, like the Sword of Damocles right in front of Penny's shocked eyes. The terrible thing about owning a sword that responds to your mental commands is that occasionally, it also responds to your subconscious desires too. Apparently, there had been a moment, ever so terrible and ever so brief, when some dark part of me would've been willing to do *anything* to carry out my plan.

It all happened so quickly that Penny didn't even have time to scream. She stared back at me with steel in her eyes. "Really?" She barked out a hollow, bitter chuckle. "This whole thing has already turned you into a monster! Keep on going down this path and you'll wind up as bad as Nick!" She threw the backpack over her shoulder and rushed out of the office.

"Penny! No! Wait! I'm sorry! I didn't mean to do that! I lost control of it for a second! I didn't mean to! I'm sorry! I would never hurt you! You know that! You've gotta believe me! Come back!" I cried out after her retreating form, but it was already too late, and the door slammed shut behind her.

I thought about chasing after her, but under the present circumstances, she'd probably think I was coming after her for a completely different, far more sinister reason.

I could barely believe what had just happened. I had never felt so low in all of my life. What was happening to me? Had I really come that close to killing Penny? How could I do that to her? I suddenly recalled the metallic tang of the barrel of my gun on my tongue with all the fondness of the memory of the sensation of a lover's caress. I thought about doing it again. In the blink of an eye, the sword swung around to the front of my own face and hovered there waiting for the command to kill. I gulped.

No, I didn't want to die, at least not yet. At least not before I had made Nick pay. I forced myself to banish away such thoughts and willed the Vermilion Avenger back into its case.

Little did I know at the time, but I would come to find out later that as Penny ran from the office and jumped into her car, she was calling Naomi on her cell phone. I would've expected her to call Randy first. I would've been wrong.

All I know about what happened next is that the conversation started out with these fateful words: "Naomi, you'd better come and get your husband right away. He's losing his goddamn mind!"

Naomi, to her credit, did exactly that. She got one of her teaching assistants to cover for her due to a "family emergency" and hurried right over to my office. Monmouth College, where she was teaching at that time (she's since moved on to Princeton) isn't all that far away, especially when you put the pedal to the metal as she is known to do. She sure burned lots of rubber getting there on that day once she caught wind of what was going on.

In the meantime, I'd busied myself by gathering Melissa's notebooks into a box on Penny's (former) desk and disconnecting her CPU from the monitor, mouse and keyboard of the office desktop. I even added my own case files and notes to the stack of materials. They were now all nicely put together, practically gift wrapped for the cops whenever they deigned to arrive. I willed the *Vermilion Avenger* back onto the hooks deeply embedded into the wall in my private office where it hung like a harmless display piece.

Inside I was still raging. Angry at myself for the things I'd said to Penny, how I'd driven her away and almost hurt her.

Hurt her? Call it what it is, you coward! Can't you even be honest with yourself? You nearly killed her! You did it without thinking, like an instinct. She's right! You're losing control! You need to stop this before it goes any further!

No! I need to get this guy. I need to make him pay for what he's done!

Oh what does it matter? Penny will probably call off the meeting with him. It's hopeless. I've already blown my best shot at nailing this scum bag and lost one of my best friends and the best damned secretary I'll ever have in the process. I've probably lost Randy too. How will I ever explain this to Naomi?

I sulked in Penny's former chair in the front part of the office. Was I more upset over what I'd done to her, or at possibly losing my best chance to kill Nick? I wish I could say for sure.

No sooner had my thoughts turned to Naomi than she came bursting through the front door, a wild look in her eyes. She was the last person I thought I'd see there that day (I'd half expected Randy to come by next and use his magic to restrain me).

"Matt, holy shit! You look like hell! I can only imagine what you've just been through." She said as she ran over and gave me a long, long, hug. Fortunately, she was smart enough to know that busting into the room with a harsher attitude wouldn't have worked. I held onto her. Clinging to her body like it was a life preserver. Indeed, she was the only thing preventing me from drowning into the depths of my own despair. It was exactly what I needed. We stood there together in silence for a long time, just holding one another. I never wanted it to end. I couldn't bear to talk to her about everything I'd just experienced, everything I'd just done. I didn't know how to own up to it. Not in front of her. I couldn't even stand to face the darkness I'd just discovered inside of myself; how could I bear to share it with the woman that I loved more than anyone else?

I started to cry. Loud, ugly sobs wracked my whole frame.

"You know, don't you?" I asked.

"I know– *everything*. Do you wanna talk about it?"

I shook my head frantically. "No, I really don't! "

"Too bad, we're going to talk about it anyway." She told me and fixed me with her infamous "look" which always brokered no further argument. I laughed then, a real heartfelt laugh for what felt like it was the first time in forever. Laughing at the wonderful familiarity of our old routines. Even in the middle of all this madness, they still prevailed. I needed that. I needed that normalcy to keep me tethered to my sanity. How desperately I needed this impossibly stubborn, brilliant, tough as nails little lady that I was fortunate enough to be able to call my wife to keep me grounded.

"Can't we just stay here like this instead, holding each other for a little longer?" I was desperate to avoid the unavoidable conversation she'd raced here to have with me.

"Don't worry. I don't intend to let you go–literally or figuratively." She assured me.

"I... I didn't mean to do that to Penny–I just lost control of the sword. You know how it is! You have to believe me! Say that you believe me!" I pleaded as I blinked back more tears.

"I understand." She breathed heavily and held me a little tighter.

She alone in all of the world *could* understand, as the only other person trained in how to use the *Vermilion Avenger,* she knew how tricky it could be. She alone understood that you had to maintain a certain mental discipline when it was nearby. The part of me that still wanted to die, that despised myself told me that I didn't deserve this kind of understanding, that I didn't deserve her. Not after how I'd failed Melissa and now Penny as well.

Naomi continued. "I also understand what it's like to deliberately kill someone too, remember? And what it's like to try and live with yourself afterwards. Believe me, you want no part of that. *I* don't want that for you either."

She did know. Years earlier, Naomi had used the *Vermilion Avenger* against a crazy cult leader named Father Steve after we'd watched him murder one of our friends right in front of us, a young witch named Autumn that we later named our daughter after. I'd never really blamed her for doing it. Steve had been part of a conspiracy that had caused a secret war amongst the Guilds. Hundreds, maybe even thousands of people had died because of his ambitions. Some of Steve's surviving victims had practically begged us to avenge them. If Naomi hadn't killed Steve first there was a very good chance that I would've done it myself. I've always wondered if I would've if she hadn't beaten me to the punch. However, she regretted it immediately. It haunted her for years afterwards. Sometimes it still did, even though when she'd traveled into the Aether and ran into Steve's spirit, she'd had a rare opportunity for closure that most people never get. It had done a lot to heal her, but sometimes the enormity of what she's done still hits her.

I just couldn't let it go that easily. "But how can I live with *myself* if I do nothing? I can't just forget about this and go on with my life like nothing happened. A young girl is dead now, dead because I couldn't save her! Dead because I was too stubborn to call on all the powers at my disposal! I have a responsibility to her, to her family, to take down her killer once and for all!"

"Matt, it's *not* your fault! You're not the bad guy here! You're not the sicko who decided to kidnap and murder a kid! But you're also not a superhero even if you've got a fancy flying sword and a suit of armor. This is real life, with real consequences! Consequences not just for you, but for your business, our marriage, our friendships and our kids! What you're contemplating doing will affect everyone around you for years to come! It's not up to us to decide these things and dole out the sentences! That kind of thing is out of our hands!"

"If it's out of our hands, then whose hands is it in? The Gods? They don't really care about what's right or wrong! Good or evil, it makes no difference to them, they see us as nothing more than a meal ticket! The universe is nothing but cold, uncaring, meaningless chaos–unless we're bold enough to impose our own kind of order onto it! There's nobody out there tipping the cosmic scales in favor of justice, there's no Karma, no rhyme or reason to anything! Even the Guilds refuse to act. They could use their power to make this world into a paradise, but they won't! They only care about their own greedy self interests. No, it *is* up to us to make things just! If not us, then who? That's all I'm trying to do here–force the world into making some sense for a change! Life might not be fair, but we've gotta try to make it fair or nothing will ever change for the better!"

"I don't completely disagree. But I'm scared for you. I know how much you're haunted by the lives you've already taken, the ones that you had no choice *but* to take just to stay alive. I sleep right next to you, I've seen you after those nightmares. I don't think you should take it to the next level like this. I'm not sure you can handle it. I think it'll break you. Shit! It almost broke me! I couldn't take that. I can't lose you! Please, don't think that I'm saying any of these things to belittle you. I don't think the fact that you're so sensitive makes you weak, not at all. One of the things that I love the most about you is that you're so compassionate. I think it's actually your greatest strength. But I can tell you from experience that when you do something like this, it doesn't change anything for the better. All the victims are still dead, and you're just left ...*diminished.* You might think that this act will satisfy the anger you're feeling right now, but it won't. Nothing ever will, only time can dull it to where it's more bearable. All that doing this will do is add to your burdens. To *our* burdens. There's no way in hell that I'm going to let you do this to yourself, or to our family! There's so much more at stake here than your own guilty feelings. Besides, I think I've come up with a better way to make sure that Melissa gets some justice. We can get this son of a bitch, we can do it *together.* We just have to be smart about *how* we do it. Please, just hear me out, give me a chance to explain my plan."

I was intrigued. I had assumed that Penny had already ruined everything or planned to do so very soon. But here was Naomi, suddenly talking like I still had a chance to take Nick down.

"What do you mean? Isn't Penny going to tell him that she can't meet him now? She was totally determined to make sure that she wasn't a party to his death in any way."

"I managed to talk her out of doing that, for now at least. She wants to bring this piece of shit down too, she just wants to do it the *right* way. She wanted to give me a chance to talk you into doing things my way instead first before she breaks things off with him for tonight."

"Okay then, I'm all ears. What's this plan of yours?"

"It's not too different from your original plan, except with less murder. You tail him from the Walmart to his home. Except you do it *astrally*. That way, there's no chance of him figuring out that you're following him and possibly losing you. Randy will be with you in the car to make sure you don't try to go after him in the real world. Once you figure out where he lives and who he is, then we tell the cops. We tell them that you had Penny arrange a meeting and that you followed him in the car from the parking lot, we leave out all the weird astral projection stuff, of course. We let the proper authorities handle this first. If they screw it up somehow, if they can't get this guy behind bars and keep him there, then and only then do we call in the Guilds. We let someone from the Houses of Assassins take care of him. There's no need to bloody your own hands with this. Give the system a chance to work before you give up on it, sometimes it actually does get things right–especially when serial killers are involved. If it fails, then we have a foolproof back up plan to make sure he never kills again."

I had to hand it to her. She'd thought of everything. A very large part of me still believed that I'd only find real satisfaction in killing Nick myself, but I had to surrender to the inescapable logic of her plan. The most important thing was to get Nick off the streets so he couldn't kill again. In the end, it didn't really matter *how* we did it, so long as it got done. Naomi's plan offered a way to do that which everyone else was presumably far more comfortable with than they were with the idea of me going off and splitting his skull open with the *Vermilion Avenger*. Why not give it a chance? Like she said, if it failed it still offered an opportunity to eliminate him down the road. "Holy shit! Yeah, it might just work! Okay, I'll give it a try. Did you think of all of that on the way over here?"

She smiled up at me with those gorgeous brown eyes of hers. A hint of mischief playing in them. "You know it! I dreamed up the whole scheme on the fly while I was trying to calm Penny down when we were talking on the phone. I left out the part about the Assassins though, I thought she might be squeamish about that." Penny might dress like a punk rocker, but she had the heart of a hippie. Honestly, in a lot of ways there isn't much of a difference when it comes down to their ideals.

The mention of Penny brought my suddenly more buoyant mood crashing back down. "I really fucked things up with her this time, didn't I? Do you think she'll ever forgive me?"

"I don't know, hon. I don't know. You'll have to ask her yourself and find out. There might be a chance, though. Even after what you did to her, she still sounded like she was worried about you. So maybe she'll come back around in the end if you kiss her ass well enough and give her a big enough raise? Maybe buy a thousand copies of her current album? Honestly, I don't know if things will ever be the same again between you two, though. It's not every day that your boss almost kills you, ya know? Talk about tension in the workplace!"

"I wouldn't blame her at all if she never wanted to come back to work for me again. I just hope that somehow the friendship can be repaired. She's been such a big part of our lives for so long now. It's hard to imagine life without her." I said regretfully.

Naomi looked up at me and kissed me. "Either way, we'll get through this *together*. We always do."

Just then, there was a knock at the door. The police had finally arrived. They didn't linger for very long, thankfully. I handed over all the stuff I'd put together for them and answered a few more questions they had for me. They thanked me for my cooperation since I technically didn't have to give them any of this stuff without a court order. I told them I'd keep them in the loop if I thought of anything else that might be helpful to them. Inside I was smiling as I said that, because I knew that very soon, if everything went according to Naomi's plan, I'd be handing them the murderer on a silver platter.

THE STING

Randy and I sat together in the confines of my car. I had parked it so that the back end faced the part of the parking lot where Nick was supposed to be parking. The reason for this was that only the back windshield and rear windows were tinted. It was illegal in NJ to have tinted windows in the front of the car. I used to have them all tinted anyway and just paid whatever tickets I would get. Then one time I got pulled over due to my tinted windows while I was in the middle of tailing someone, which caused me to completely lose them. I was so pissed off by that incident that I swore I'd never let that happen again. I had the front tint removed the very next day.

Randy was in the back seat scanning the parking lot with a pair of binoculars that were small enough to easily fit in a pocket but were ridiculously powerful. Hopefully the tint would make him hard to spot doing something so suspicious. It was already dark outside, but the powerful lights in the parking lot kept it fairly well lit.

It was getting closer to the time when Nick was supposed to show up. We didn't know if he'd decide to show up early or not to case the place, so we weren't taking any chances. I knew that if I was him, I'd be a little suspicious that I was being set up. But then again, I was assigning rational ideas to someone who seemed to be behaving more like a crazed animal. Then again, if he really was a serial killer, he was likely to be pretty clever in his own sick way, or else he wouldn't have been able to get away with murder over and over again.

I wondered if he'd been hidden somewhere near the park where he'd dumped Melissa's body so he could watch when it was found. I'd heard that these kinds of creeps sometimes got off on that sort of thing. If that was the case, there was a chance that he might recognize my car. I wished I'd thought of this sooner and switched vehicles with Naomi. Or maybe I was just being too paranoid?

The thought of Naomi made me recall how she had taken possession of the *Vermilion Avenger* back from me before leaving my office. This was as much to keep me from using it consciously or unconsciously and slipping up with it again. She'd even taken all the guns from the office. It had hurt me a little that my own wife felt the need to take these precautions, but again I had to bow to the logic of it all. I had been out of control today, in ways that nobody else even knew about. Was it really so unreasonable that I shouldn't be trusted with any weapons right now?

Randy hadn't given me too much of a hard time over what had happened between me and Penny. In fact, he'd barely mentioned it. He seemed to be more focused on the situation at hand. I was grateful for that. It was more than I deserved. He had every right to be mad and disappointed in me, but if he was, he did a damned fine job of not showing it. As I got more and more nervous that Nick would get cold feet at the last minute, I asked him to text Penny and make sure that Nick hadn't sent her any new messages where he tried to bow out. She reported that as far as she could tell, everything was all still set for tonight. In fact, he'd sent her a message about an hour ago to make sure that *she* would show up. She said he seemed quite eager to meet her.

Yeah, I'll bet you are, you sick fuck! I thought.

I was happy that Penny was still cooperating with me on this whole thing. I hoped that I could convince her to return to work eventually. She was quite literally irreplaceable. I'd had to hire temps to do her job when she went on tour with her band and had yet to find anyone who ever came close to doing as good of a job as she did. I knew that I wouldn't even be so close to nailing this jerk if it wasn't for all the work she had done in finding out about him and baiting this trap. Had I really told her that I didn't need her? Had I really been that stupid? She was right–we all do say idiotic, cruel things that we don't really mean when we get too caught up in the heat of the moment.

"This might be him!" Randy reported excitedly from the back seat.

"Can you read the license plates?" I asked.

"No, there's too much shit in the way." I could practically hear the frown in my partner's voice then.

"Okay, I'm gonna do my thing and go astral." I said, taking a deep breath and laying my head back against the headrest.

You have to put yourself into a trance to astrally project. The secret society of magic users that Randy belongs to, the Temple of the Old Gods, had long ago perfected a very quick and easy technique for doing so that just about anyone could learn. I was a little rusty at it, as I find the whole thing to be a pretty spooky experience, and I rarely ever do it, but it's like that old cliche about riding a bike–you never really forget how to do it.

Within moments I was looking down on my sleeping body. I floated down through the seat so that I was next to Randy. He could see and hear me in this form even though most normal people can't. It's a wizard thing, apparently.

"Where is he?"

Randy pointed in the general direction of a row of cars about three rows ahead of us. Then he muttered a quick spell that turned his finger into a kind of laser pointer, a beam of light extending from his fingertip and out to the car in question. It was invisible, of course, to anyone who wasn't already on the astral plane like I was or attuned to it mentally. This parking lot was just barely out of range of the current location of the Orb (back in my house on the opposite side of town) so Randy was able to work his magic.

"Thanks, pal."

"Good luck, Matt!" He wished me as I moved my astral body through the back windshield and out of my car, following Randy's beam of light.

As scary as astral projection can be, it's also undeniably exhilarating. Exhilarating in the same way that a good rollercoaster ride is both terrifying and exciting. Here I was, basically flying along like some sort of a superhero! How could some small part of me not find the fulfillment of this old childhood dream to be anything less than exhilarating? It was always a little exciting no matter how many times I did it or how grim the circumstances might be, and right now the circumstances were about as grim as they could get.

Another danger, at least in my eyes, of doing this too often is that it can (according to Randy) boost one's own natural psychic sensitivity over time. This is all well and good if you're a wizard or a witch, from what little I understand of such matters, their ability to successfully cast a spell depends to some extent on developing this psychic potential. However, if you're just a regular guy like me who does his level best to try to ignore all the weirdness around him and have something resembling a normal life, becoming more psychically attuned is something you want to avoid. Sure, being more psychic can make you a better detective, but I prefer to do things more conventionally.

I suddenly realized that this kind of limited thinking is exactly what caused me to fail Melissa like I had, and I cursed myself. I wondered if I had been ignoring some of the clues that the psychic part of my nature had been trying to give me? Perhaps that's why I'd had that awful nightmare about Melissa a few nights earlier? It had certainly turned out to be tragically prophetic. Perhaps this was also what had really led me to the park this morning? Had that really been just this morning? It felt so far away now. If only I had listened to these gut instincts sooner! Randy was right, you should never ignore your instincts. Even after knowing him for so many years, I'd somehow failed to properly absorb the full importance of this lesson, and it had cost a girl her life!

I tried to set aside these self-recriminations as I neared Nick's car. Time to focus on the task at hand, the here and now. This was something else that Randy was always trying to remind me to do.

As I approached the car, I made sure to memorize the license plate number. It was a Jersey plate. I'd just caught him in the first of his many lies. I flew right through Nick's windshield and settled down to sit next to him in the passenger seat. I studied his profile as I watched him wait. He was singing along tunelessly to something by the Backstreet Boys while he waited. *Yeah, he's a real freak, alright,* I thought as I came to understand that it wasn't the radio, he had an entire CD of theirs that he was playing. It was surreal to think that I was sitting right next to the person who had caused so much harm. It was even stranger to think that someone so goofy and innocent looking could do such terrible things. You really can't judge a book by its cover.

He was far younger looking than I'd expected, but then again as I've already said, the older I get the harder it becomes for me to tell this sort of thing with much accuracy. Everyone younger than me begins to look like a baby. He certainly had a smooth, cleanly shaven baby face. I began to wonder if he really *was* a freshman in college. He could pass for it. This made me wonder if I was barking up the wrong tree and the killer was someone else? No! Everything pointed to it being him, this is what my entire being was screaming at me. Besides, it was far too much of a coincidence that Melissa disappeared the same night she was supposed to meet him, and that her body was dumped in the same park where the meeting was supposed to take place.

As he became increasingly irritated with the fruitless waiting, he did some things that reaffirmed my faith that I was on the right track after all.

"Looks like the little bitch is standing me up!" He growled in a low voice that dripped with contempt. He then hammered on his steering wheel a few times with such force it's a wonder he didn't bust the steering column. As he did so he bit down on one corner of his mouth so hard that blood trickled down from his lip and down the side of his mouth, making him look like some sort of a vampire, which in a way, I suppose he was. He didn't bother to wipe it away. Instead, he flipped back some of the long strands of brown hair that had fallen in front of his face during his little temper tantrum and started breathing heavily. He stared up at the ceiling of his car for a few minutes, checked the time again, flipped over his awful CD, then drove off.

Oh yeah, he's a real piece of work! I thought smugly as he left the parking lot behind, blissfully unaware that he'd picked up a passenger after all, just not the kind he expected. As we drove along, my attention kept on being drawn by a sound I would hear periodically coming from the backseat. I looked behind myself and saw a duffel bag sitting there, within easy reach of him. The sounds I was hearing were the sounds of the contents jostling around inside. I literally stuck my head inside the bag to examine what it held.

There was no light in there. But in your astral body you don't really need light to be able to "see" things. These items did give off a sort of slight luminescence though, their own kind of ghastly red aura. Even to a novice at this sort of thing like myself, it was obvious what this meant: these objects had already been put to a nefarious purpose and the psychic residue of those dark deeds clung to them palpably. There were a bunch of wire ties, a rag that was likely soaked in chloroform, a box cutter and some duct tape. There was also some rope. With a start I understood that what I was looking at was this creep's "kill kit"! There was no doubt now that "Nick" was our man.

My anger at Nick was renewed by this grisly discovery. How I longed to yank on the steering wheel and send him careening into a tree. If I could concentrate hard enough, I might be able to do it too. It was very difficult (especially for someone like me), but it was possible to manipulate physical objects in this form. But I had promised Naomi to do this the "right way" and I didn't want to disappoint her any more than I already had. There were other good reasons for seeing this guy taken into custody too. If he died now, he'd just be another random victim of a traffic accident. Melissa's parents wouldn't get whatever small degree of closure they might be able to squeeze out of the knowledge that the person responsible for slaughtering their daughter had been caught. Also, if he had any other victims, I'd be denying those families that same opportunity. These dirtbags usually gave up info on previous victims once apprehended, some of them taking

TALES FROM A DEAD END WORLD – VOLUME TWO

a sick sort of pride in their murders. There was no reason to think that this guy wouldn't do the same in time. He could help close lots of cold cases. I had to concentrate on cold, hard facts like that to keep myself under control.

After driving for about 40 minutes (we were *definitely* not in Highland Park, we were farther north) we found ourselves pulling up to a pair of large wrought iron gates. The creep rolled down his window and punched a security code into a keypad. I noted with some degree of grim amusement that the code was "0666"--at least the guy knew what he really was. The gates swung open, and he drove up a winding path towards a large mansion of a home. Even in the darkness I could see that the grounds were not being kept up. The grass was quite tall and looked like it hadn't been cut in months. The rows of hedges that we passed by had also obviously not been trimmed recently. Nick pulled into a large garage which held several other cars, quite a few of them vintage. It was an impressive collection. I'm no gearhead, but even I can recognize a '57 Chevy and Model T when I see one. As he cut the engine off, the sounds of the Backstreet Boys mercifully came to an end, which no doubt was contributing to my own murderous mood. He reached into his backseat and took his "murder kit" bag with him as he left the garage and entered the house.

The inside of the house wasn't much better than the outside. This home would've been impressive at one time, but now it almost looked like it should've been on one of those hoarder shows. Okay, I'm exaggerating a bit, it wasn't quite *that* bad, but it was a mess, with bits of trash just thrown on the floor. It was a mix of crushed soda cans and cardboard boxes for such culinary treasures as "hot pockets" and other equally unhealthy snack foods. Two things were immediately obvious to me from what I had seen so far: Nick lived in this huge palace of a house all by himself and he also had no idea how to cook anything that didn't involve shoving something into a microwave for a few minutes. Here was someone who was used to having all these things done for him and suddenly had to make do by himself. If there had once been servants, he must've gotten rid of them all. This made a certain degree of sense; he couldn't have lots of potential witnesses hanging around to whatever atrocities he committed within these walls. Firing the staff must've happened in the relatively recent past, otherwise the condition of the place would've been far worse. Or maybe he just had someone come in periodically to clean it up?

I wondered how it was that someone who looked so young had this place all to himself. He didn't look old enough to have the money to afford a place like this on his own yet. Was he some sort of an orphan that had inherited the place? Where were his parents?

I followed him through the building into a large library. This room was relatively unscathed, which showed how little time he spent in it. There was a large fireplace in the room, and I spied several old family photos on the mantelpiece. Here, at last, were the missing parents. There was a large painting of someone who I now recognized as being his father hanging over it all. From the bookshelf, Nick pulled on the spine of *The Count of Monte Cristo.* A section of the wall slid aside, just like in some old movie or an episode of *Scooby Doo* revealing a hidden passageway.

Holy cliché, Batman! I thought to myself as he disappeared down the throat of the murky tunnel. I wondered if he was the one who had the secret tunnel installed or if it had been the work of his parents or a previous owner? The hidden entrance began to slide shut, temporarily forgetting that I could pass through solid objects in my current form, I instinctively rushed forward before it could seal shut behind me.

The tunnel opened up into a room that looked as though it had been used as a vault in the past. There were shelves built into the walls and a large safe dominated one of them. The walls were splattered in dried blood and macabre trophies decorated the shelves. There were bits of jewelry and severed body parts floating in thirteen jars of formaldehyde. Mostly they were ears, but occasionally I spotted a finger (with a ring still on it). There was also a tongue and even an eye. They were all arranged quite neatly, in stark contrast to the disarray of the rest of the house. There was a high backed wooden antique chair in the center of the room. It had been bolted to the floor and leather straps were attached to the arm rests and one of the legs. Next to it was a metal table filled with whips, chains, scalpels and knives of all sizes.

The place is a goddamned torture dungeon! I thought in disgust. A fresh wave of fury shot through me as I realized that some of the blood on these walls was Melissa's and one of those ears undoubtedly belonged to her. What torments had she suffered while she sat in that chair? Had death seemed like a mercy when it finally came?

He set down his murder kit on that table and sighed heavily, obviously disappointed that he didn't have a new victim to place in that chair tonight as planned. I had seen enough. I already had memorized this address when we pulled up to the gate, which the street number prominently displayed on a metal plate. I had his license plate number too. I didn't want to hang around any longer in this horrible place, with this horrible person. It then occurred to me that I still didn't know his real name. I should probably try to find a piece of mail or something with his name on it, just in case the plates were registered to someone else. Moreover, I felt like I needed to know who he really was to satisfy my own curiosity.

He was still standing in the center of the room, his hands on his hips now, surveying his collection of pickled body parts like a king looking at his subjects. That's when I saw her. The ghost of a tall, thin woman with somewhat frizzy black hair materialized from out of nowhere and threw a punch at his face.

He didn't even blink. The ghost howled in anger, then looked over at me with a look of surprise.

Great, I've been spotted by her.

Ghosts were one more reason why I hated astral projection. They were all over the place, and meeting one was usually very upsetting. Ah well, maybe this one would have some useful information for me? That would only work if her mind was still coherent enough to answer my questions. Oftentimes when dealing with ghosts they were too confused to get anything very useful out of them, especially the longer they'd been dead. I thought it was safe to assume that she was likely one of his previous victims.

"You can see me?" She asked me in a shocked voice.

"Yeah. Hi, uh my name is Matt." I replied awkwardly as I watched Nick decide to leave the room. She tried to kick him on his way out, her leg passing through him ineffectually.

"My name is Millie, Millie Craighead. Did he get you too, Matt? I've seen him get so many people." She said with melancholy.

"No, I'm a detective. I was hired to find Melissa and that led me here."

Her eyes widened at the mention of Melissa. "She was just here, the poor girl. I saw what he did to her, well some of it. After a while I can't stand to watch anymore. I always try to stop him, but I can't do anything to him! I can't hurt him back no matter how hard I try! I'm just cursed to watch and watch and never be able to stop him! I tried to save her, I really did! I just couldn't!" She didn't seem to fully grasp *why* she couldn't hurt him. See what I mean about them being confused? It's like one minute they understand that they're dead, then the next instant they forget again.

"I know what you mean. I...failed to save her too. I'm hoping that I can do something now to stop him for good. What can you tell me about him? Do you know his real name?"

"Thomas Rey is his real name. What is there to know about him other than that he's a sick little motherfucker? He likes to pick up working girls like me, flash them a thick wad of cash, then bring 'em back here and do *awful* things to them. That's how he got me. Lately he's been using his computer upstairs to find new girls. I think he thinks that's safer for him. It's been happening more and more too. Like he can't get enough."

I nodded. Her description of herself as a "working girl" told me that she had been a prostitute before he made her his victim. I was reminded of the cop at the crime scene mentioning a prostitute that had been found with a missing ear recently. Had that been Millie? From where I stood, I couldn't tell if she still had both of her ears or not. Also, ghosts were strange in that sometimes they looked like they did at the moment of death and sometimes they didn't. I don't pretend to understand what determines how they appear to other people. Even if her specter had been missing an ear, it wouldn't tell me if she was the unfortunate victim he'd left behind in New Brunswick. Removing ears seemed to be part of his MO, judging by the number of ears I had seen floating in jars across the room from myself. Picking up prostitutes was also part of his pattern, which wasn't so unusual for serial killers, who often preyed on vulnerable people who they thought wouldn't be missed or valued much by society. She could be a recent victim or one of his first. Since ghosts had a very skewed perception of the passage of time, I doubted that she could reliably tell me either. However, she seemed to be fairly coherent, with most of her mental faculties still about her, which made me think that she must be a relatively recent victim. I wondered if any of his other victims were still hanging around here too? Trying to exact a vengeance on him that they could never get.

"I don't see how you can do anything more to him than I can, Matt. Not when we're both stuck like this." She complained, demonstrating an impressive understanding of her current situation that many ghosts lacked. "God knows I've tried. I've tried to strangle him in his sleep, tried to throw these knives at him, I've tried all kinds of things, but I just can't get him."

"I'm not quite like you. It's hard to explain, but I'm still alive. See this golden cord that's coming out of my belly button? It connects me to my body." I pulled on a luminous cord of light that protruded from my abdomen and stretched back behind me disappearing through the walls of the dungeon.

"I'm going to wake myself up soon and tell the cops all about this place. There's plenty of evidence here to link him to his crimes. Don't worry, Millie, justice is coming for him, very soon."

"Shit!" She swore, "Just what kind of a detective are you?"

"The kind that can finally make him pay for what he's done." I said with a confidence I didn't completely feel. I think

I was putting on a brave face for her benefit, hoping that her tortured soul would draw some comfort from the idea that the monster that had taken her life would finally get what was coming to him.

She shook her head sadly and I caught a fleeting glimpse of a ragged hole on the side of her head where an ear should've been. "No. I don't know that he could ever *really* be made to pay for all the suffering he's caused, not in a thousand years."

"Well, all I can do is try. And I *will* get this madness to stop, I promise you that. Melissa will be his last victim." I was sure of myself as I made that promise. I also made another promise to myself–to send Randy back here to make sure that Millie and the ghosts of any other victims that might be around here moved on to the Afterlife. I might not approve of the place, but it was still preferable to staying on this plane of existence while your soul slowly degraded like a corrupted computer file.

"Goodbye, Millie and thanks for your help. It was nice meeting you." I said. Before she could reply, I closed my eyes and forced myself back into wakefulness. There was an odd rushing sensation as I felt my golden cord yank me backwards at a terrific speed and I was blasted back into my physical body. The next time I opened my eyes, they were my real eyes. I let out a deep breath as I came to. My head pounded. Another annoying thing about astral projection was that sometimes you felt all woozy and hung over right afterwards, especially when you brought yourself out of that state far too quickly like I had just done. It was like being a diver with a case of the bends, except the pain was in your head.

"How long was I out?" I asked Randy, who was now sitting beside me.

"About two hours." He answered.

This was close to what I had figured. It was difficult to gauge the passage of time in the physical world when on the astral plane, I was happy to note that I was getting better at figuring out the time differential between the two layers of reality.

"Quick! Write down this information before I forget it!" I urged him, then regurgitated the name "Thomas Rey", his address and license plate number, along with a description of the outside of his house. Randy dutifully wrote down everything I told him on a notepad he produced from his jacket pocket.

I also had him write down the name "Millie Craighead". I couldn't share that name with the police right away, as I couldn't think of a normal sounding explanation for how I'd know it, but I intended to research it for myself later on. If he had any victims that the authorities couldn't identify as being

Millie, then perhaps I could drop them an anonymous tip about her disappearance being linked to this case? It was worth a shot. I was determined not to let Millie down either. I wouldn't let her be forgotten.

I had decided that I'd tell the cops that I'd parked my car outside the gates of Thomas Rey's not so stately estate and scaled the gate. I would tell them that I'd watched him enter the secret tunnel that led to his dungeon through a window. While this implicates me in trespassing, I don't think that under the circumstances, anyone will really care, and I can handle whatever penalties I might have to face for it. The important thing was to make sure that they found that room when they searched his place and the treasure trove of evidence it housed that not only tied him to the murders but would also hopefully help identify his victims too.

"This is really good stuff, Matt! I think we've got him!" Randy smiled as he finished writing down what I was saying and put his notepad away.

"Thanks. Yeah, now all I have to do is figure out how to tell the cops about it."

THE RESOLUTION

As it turned out, it wasn't too difficult to tell the cops. I called the same detectives that had come by my office earlier that day and told them all about my little sting operation. They were understandably pissed at me for not clueing them into it when I'd seen them earlier. I explained that I was afraid that they'd discourage me from going forward with it, but I didn't feel that I could abandon the plan when it was so close to fruition. They still felt the need to condescendingly lecture me about getting too involved in what was now a police matter and how even a well-meaning "amateur" (that one stung!) could've fucked up everything and caused the perp to flee town if he'd spotted me tailing him. Underneath all their self-righteousness though, I could tell that they were secretly pleased that I'd already done all the hard work for them.

For whatever reason, tracing the IP address was taking longer than they'd hoped. I had at least given them a starting point in the meantime. They immediately had his house put under twenty-four-hour surveillance while they awaited confirmation that the computer that had been communicating with Melissa's was indeed at that address.

That didn't happen until nearly three days later for some God forsaken reason.

It turns out that he couldn't wait that long to go back out on the hunt again.

Whatever frenzy of excitement he'd worked himself up into at the prospect of claiming another victim that night had been unexpectedly stymied, and he couldn't just let it end like that. He was determined to still get his prize one way or the other. He just had to do something with all that pent up energy, to release it. I found out that after I'd left him, but thankfully not before he had police watching his house, he went back out again. The cops trailed him up to a particularly seedy section of Newark known for prostitution. When he picked up a young girl off the streets, the cops tailing him called in the local PD and they arrested him. The discovery of his "murder kit" in the backseat was the icing on the cake. I like to think that although I failed to save Melissa, my actions that night did save the life of the young girl he picked up in Newark.

The police now had more probable cause to search his place than just the testimony of some maverick, trespassing PI. Thomas Rey's home was searched, and the torture dungeon promptly located, which gave them more than enough reason to hold him longer.

He was rich enough to hire the best attorneys, and if he'd been smart, he would've shut his mouth and lawyered up right away. However, pride ultimately proved to be his downfall, too. Once he'd been caught, he couldn't wait to start bragging about his many crimes. His trial was an unusually swift one, and he was eventually sentenced to life several times over. He didn't last long in the prison system. A year into his time inside he was killed by another prisoner in a petty squabble over cigarettes.

It couldn't have happened to a nicer guy. I take no pride in reporting that I smiled at the news. It's a terrible thing to be happy about the demise of another human being, no matter how sick they are. It's barbaric. I know that, but I'd be lying if I tried to pretend that the knowledge that he was now gone forever from this Earth and could never get out and hurt anyone else didn't give me some small degree of satisfaction. The thing is that it is a *small* degree of satisfaction. A *very* small degree. Would it have really been any more satisfying if I had done it myself? I doubt it. Just like Naomi told me, the anger is still there whenever I think about him. Hot, fresh and visceral. The anger never completely goes away, time just dulls the edge of the knife a little, but it's still always sharp enough to cut you if you let it.

I don't like to talk about him. I feel like we spend too much time talking about these kinds of people and not enough time remembering the victims. I wish I could forget him. Yet I suppose I *must* talk about him, it's all part of this therapy– confronting my feelings about him that I keep buried and refuse to deal with. That is part of the point of reliving all of this, of writing this all down, isn't it? Okay, so here we go I suppose.

Who was Thomas Rey? Much has been written about him in the years since, probably too much, and yet solid answers still elude us as to what turned him into the monster that he was. Even though I wish I could forget that he ever existed, that he'd never touched my life, I also can't help but be fascinated with this question too. It's like passing a bad car wreck on the side of the road. You know you shouldn't look, but you can't help yourself from doing it.

Despite liking to brag about his "work" as he called it, he never gave any straight answers as to whatever meaning there was behind it. He was known for giving many conflicting, contradictory statements on the matter.

He was possessed of a deep-seated misogyny. Some people point to what was, by all accounts, a badly strained relationship with his mother as the possible origin of this. I personally don't go in for all that Freudian shit, so while I think that might've been a contributing factor, I feel like there's gotta be something more to it. Some of the things he said indicated some kind of trauma from a previous, likely abusive relationship that he never discussed. He said that he took tongues because "it stopped all the lies", ring fingers were to stop "broken promises", the eyes because he "never felt seen". His favorite were the ears. The ears had a double meaning for him. They were removed because he "never felt truly heard", but also as a twisted homage to Vincent Van Gogh. Somehow, I don't think Vince would've approved.

That's the other thing about him, the guy was an art nut. If I had explored his house further, I would've seen evidence of this all over the walls. The collection of art in the mansion surpassed the collection of vintage cars that I'd seen in the garage (which had belonged to his father). Apparently, he inherited this love of fine art from his late maternal grandfather (who was also the source of most of his inherited wealth) with whom he had been uncommonly close to. Art had been his grandfather's passion, and he was known as being a great collector and dealer in his time. At one time there had been some nasty rumors amongst the servants that his grandfather was his *actual* father, and that he was the product of an incestuous union. Some researchers have also seized upon this as being the source of tension between Thomas and his mother. Who knows? All these people brought their dirty little secrets with them to the grave.

Thomas had once had a younger brother, who had died when he was still a toddler. He would later claim that this had been his first victim, that he had pushed him into the pool in the backyard when nobody else was around. It would be a few more years before he would kill again, his next victim being a fellow student at the boarding school he attended.

He really hit his stride as he moved into his college years. Despite his unusually youthful appearance, he was actually twenty-five years old when he was arrested. Up until recently, he'd been a grad student with a degree in art history. He moved from university to university frequently and he'd been all around the country. The prostitutes that could often be found in these college towns were usually his prey, simply because they were convenient and wouldn't be as missed. However, whenever it was possible, whenever he thought that he could get away with it, he preferred to get his hands on a fellow student. This is why he transferred schools so often, leaving town whenever the pile of bodies he left in his wake was beginning to become too conspicuous, whenever there was danger of others seeing a pattern beginning to emerge.

His parents eventually became frustrated with all this constant moving from school to school, and the fact that he seemed to be a "career student" who would seemingly never be finished with school and move on to a real career. They began threatening to cut him off unless he settled down and finished what he started. It wasn't too long after that that they ended up dead themselves.

Thomas had been researching slow acting poisons that were so obscure that they usually weren't even screened for by toxicologists. When he found some that mimicked the symptoms of other diseases, he went to work. He used his money to obtain these rare poisons, then moved back home and began surreptitiously adding them to his parents' food and drink. Mom was the first to go, then a few months later, dad too. He was clever enough to find poisons that mimicked the symptoms of two different fatal diseases. If anyone found these deaths to be suspicious, he either bought their silence, or silenced them himself.

With his parents now out of the way, he fired all of the full-time staff at what was now his mansion and things really kicked into overdrive. Whereas in the past he had killed only a few times a year, it now became a monthly thing, then a weekly thing. Without having to worry about being caught by his parents and with full access to their fortune, he felt unstoppable and started getting bolder. At first, he would hide or destroy the bodies, but now he displayed them openly, taunting the authorities to stop him. It was all some kind of sick game to him. He dropped out of school and discovered the internet as a way of finding new victims. He devoted himself to it fully. Bringing death became his new reason for living.

Another peculiar thing that he said once in an interview has become the subject of much speculation amongst those who get obsessed with studying killers. Despite never being diagnosed with schizophrenia, he claimed to hear voices, or rather one *specific* voice which urged him to kill. This voice had a name, and that name was Benjamin Crooke. He said that he owned a painting made by Crooke that he had inherited from his beloved grandfather, and that Crooke communicated to him through it. This portrait was never found amongst his possessions, nor was there any record of it in his grandfather's papers. Yet above Thomas's bed there was a spot where a painting had obviously once hung and been removed.

At first, everyone dismissed this story as just a desperate attempt to gain leniency through an insanity defense. Then he defied all expectations by never seeking such a defense. In time, researchers discovered that there had in fact once been a portrait painter in Victorian London by the name of Benjamin Crooke who had gone insane and became one of the first serial killers of the modern era, predating Jack the Ripper by several decades. Crooke was once notorious, as much for the odd circumstances of his execution as for his body count. A strange incident happened at the gallows when he was hung–his still twitching body was said to have disappeared into thin air in full view of a large crowd. The conventional wisdom at the time was that "the devil couldn't wait to claim him as his own". For years Crooke was dismissed as being nothing more than a barely remembered urban legend and there was scant evidence of his existence remaining. The records of his arrest and trial were destroyed in the Blitz of London during the Second World War. Most of what we know about him comes from the account of a mental patient from the early 20th Century who showed up from out of nowhere claiming to be him. This was impossible however, since this was a young man at the time and if Crooke had still been alive, he would've been close to 100 years old. However, this patient knew many details of Crooke's life that were confirmed by the hospital staff using records that now no longer survive.

The strangest thing about all of this Benjamin Crooke business is that once when I was discussing it with a close friend of mine, April Sommardahl (a witch who is also the wife of Randy's mentor Wendy) she had an extreme reaction to that name. She told me that during her whole childhood she'd been haunted by a dark spirit that claimed to be behind a string of personal tragedies that had plagued her back then. This same spirit had also claimed to be Benjamin Crooke. She told me that with the help of another witch, she eventually vanquished him, and he had never troubled her again. But this whole incident with Thomas Rey made me wonder–was the spirit of Benjamin Crooke still out there somewhere causing mayhem? Had it corrupted Thomas' grandfather first and then him? If so, then how much of what Thomas Rey did was he ultimately responsible for? Or is Benjamin Crooke, like the Devil, just another scapegoat for the potential for evil that dwells inside us all?

I know now that evil is real. I also know now that it lives inside of me too. I got as close as I ever feared to come to giving in to it during this whole episode. I also know that I didn't have any Devil or Benjamin Crooke whispering in my ear. I only have myself to blame for my own actions, and in many ways, that's the most difficult cross to bear of them all. If evil spirits are real, and do sometimes influence certain people, then all they're doing is taking advantage of some sickness or weakness that's already there and giving them a little push, a push right off the edge into full blown insanity. I know now from bitter experience that it doesn't take much to fall off that edge once you've been there, teetering on the precipice.

The good news is that if you're on the edge like that, if you're fortunate enough to be surrounded by good people and positive influences, they can just as easily help to pull you away from that awful cliff as any negative ones can to push you off of it. I was lucky enough to have an amazing wife and friends that knew how to talk to me and were there for me when I needed them the most. They saved me from myself. Not everyone is that fortunate.

In the end, I wonder if that's the only real difference between me and a "monster" like Thomas Rey? The presence of strong positive influences in our lives? We like to think that people like him aren't human by calling them things like "monsters" but the truth, the really difficult truth that we always try to hide away from, is that they're just as human as we are. They're not unfathomable, inhuman demons. They're human beings like us that do monstrous, unforgivable things. We're more like them than we ever want to believe. It's a difficult pill to swallow, trust me on that one.

In the end, I'm glad that I didn't kill him myself. His capture did help to close a bunch of cold cases and gave many families the answers they needed to move forwards. This included the family of a young street walker named Millie Craighead (whose once restless spirit Randy did eventually help to put to rest). If I had just executed Thomas, whatever good ultimately came out of his confessions might not have ever happened. Also, I'm glad that I didn't open the door into the dark part of my own soul that I'd briefly gazed into any wider. Killing him could've easily blown that door right off its hinges. I still hate him, as much for what he did to Melissa as for what he made me see in myself. I know that somehow I need to figure out how to let go of all that anger before it eats me up. I'll get there someday, it's a process, as they say.

I'm especially grateful to still have Penny in my life after all this mess. I was too much of a coward to try and call her up the night we had our blowup and apologize, but when I came back into the office the next morning, she was back in her usual spot behind the desk again as if nothing ever happened. She's more than I deserve.

"You're back?" I gasped in astonishment.

"Of course I'm back, Matt. That's what family does, they come back because they don't give up on each other." She said it as if it was the most obvious thing in the world. I suppose it should've been.

I'm not ashamed to admit that I lost it right at that moment, I started crying like a baby. I *did* have that talk with her then that I'd been avoiding. I apologized a thousand times. I gave her a raise.

And yes, I *did* buy a thousand copies of her latest album, briefly making it move up the charts ever so slightly.

I really am impossibly lucky to have the people around me that I have in my life. I sometimes find it hard to live with myself, but they make it a little easier. They see something good in me that I often can't, and I'll always love them all for that.

TRUTH IS THEIR BUSINESS

Matt and Naomi are quite the pair
She peers into the past to see what lies buried there
Wishing to discover how we all got here
For in our prior follies always lies a lesson to illustrate where
in the future we must steer
To avoid fresh disasters of our own manufacture which
always loom so near
Matt wants to understand how
Is it that we came to be who we are right now?
What is it that truly drives us and makes us tick?
Why does the human spirit seem to be so sick?
Inside us all he sees both an angels and a demon
Bereft of all kindness and reason
Why then, is it to that cruel demon within
That we so often are compelled to give in?
Both wish to understand what it means to be a person in this
too jagged life
Which often pokes, jabs and cuts just like a knife
United in solving this great mystery,
Yet from different angles
Like quantum particles they are entangled
He is forever her man and she is forever his wife
Penny's head is endlessly racing, she seldom ever finds any
sleep
Seeking to discover the secrets from herself which her heart
does keep
In her mind there is always song
In this form, she tries to unravel the countless answers for
which she longs

A loyal companion, she makes sure all the others always have what they need
Taking care of them she sees as her noblest deed
Whatever the danger, whatever the stakes
She will swallow her fear to do what it takes
To protect the surrogate families she makes
Randy is like Jesus the historical man reborn
Against being seen as some kind of savior this time he is forsworn
Things didn't work out so well the last time around when he preached to love one another
Like you would a brother or your own mother
Too easily can such messages be misused, abused
Once they have been loosed
Better not to make any such heavenly report
Lest its meaning the unscrupulous seize upon for their own ends to distort
Yet, if there was something he would like to convey
It would be this which he has to say:
Don't look to any God for all your problems to mend
Upon them you cannot fully depend
Instead, look to yourself, look to a friend
For true divinity lies within
Stop this obsession with who has the most sin
Don't treat eternal bliss like a contest you can win
These answers are always all around
In every moment they abound
In every touch, sight and sound
Spiritual truths are subjective
Not like a science, so objective
There is no one size to which all will fit
As the wise Madonna once said "beauty's where you find it"

Follow your individual passions to solve this case
That's the key to the liberation of the whole human race
Now get out of my face
Leave me be, I just want to play the bass
Far away to some mysterious other world have Matt and his
friends all now gone
Just like Arthur to his Avalon
And like that Once and Future King they may all yet one day
return
When deep in the human heart a new mystery does burn

MATT

Come, seeker of truth

Redemption is what you need

Found in a rescue

BELLA LUGOSI SAVED MY LIFE LAST NIGHT

I lay face down, immobile in my bed, the covers thrown over my head, as was my fashion. If I don't do that then I might see things, things that I don't want to see. In this case, the covers failed to shield me from that fate. I could still see the bad thing in my bedroom. I didn't need my eyes; I could see it as clear as day in the theater of my mind.

It seemed harmless enough as it stood at my bedside, innocent even. Indeed, to many

people it might seem to be the very picture of innocence. It was a little girl, in appearance no older than seven or eight years of age, but this too was a lie. She was black, with her hair in two long braids with those colorful little balls holding them in place. She wore a dress that went down a little past her knees and reminded me of something Raggedy Ann would wear, or maybe Alice from those Lewis Carroll books. Her hands were clasped behind her back as she regarded me, lying there helpless before her. She was holding me down with her power, the force of her mind pinning me to the mattress, unable to flip over, unable even to cry out.

This little girl was no little girl. She was a vampire. I knew it as certainly as I knew any fact in a dream. *Was this a dream?* Hard to tell. The fact that I was questioning its reality would seem to argue against it, but stranger things have happened. If anyone was going to have a ridiculously meta kind of dream, it would be me.

I also knew, with great certainty, that I was to become her next victim. That she was just toying with me like how a cat toys with a mouse before devouring it. Savoring my rising terror at my own helplessness, like it was a finely aged wine. It's why she'd roused me just enough to make me aware of my hopeless predicament. It was insidious. Diabolical, even.

I could respect that. *Well played kid, well played.*

Now she was just going to make me wait in dreadful anticipation of my own end. For I also knew it was to be the end. I wasn't going to be joining the ranks of the Undead tonight. There wasn't a recruitment drive going on right now. I wasn't a prospective member of the Children of the Night, I was just a takeout meal. A bit of fast food to be consumed, discarded and ultimately forgotten. Can you distinguish one visit to McDonalds as being especially outstanding in deliciousness as any other? Of course not. It was like that. I was just another Happy Meal. Not even one that came with a cool toy. No more memorable than any other meal. Look, if you're about to become someone's dinner, it's at least some small comfort to know that you'll live on in their memory as being especially tasty, but I knew I wouldn't have even the minimal comfort of that dubious distinction. This was all terribly routine to her.

I was terribly routine.

It was such a shame, I rather liked to think that I had a lot to offer the organization in terms of sheer panache. I'd make a damned fine vampire! But nobody cared. No one could see my potential in this field, and honestly, that's what hurt most of all. Not the fact that I was about to die, but the sting of rejection at not even being considered for membership!

There's nothing quite as humbling as staring down the barrel of your own insignificance. What a way to die! At least my death would be somewhat puzzling and memorable. Exsanguinated in my own bed! That was a stylish way to go. Nothing run of the mill about that. I just hoped my poor housemate wouldn't catch the blame for it. I knew she hadn't visited him yet, and through our mental link, I could feel that she had no plans to do so, preferring to dine on me instead. That, at least, made me feel a little more special.

She stepped forth, perhaps tiring a bit of the game. Of the crushing weight of my emotional neediness even in the face of death.

That's when he appeared, quite literally, from out of nowhere. My personal savior, drenched in black satin. The Ghost of Bela Lugosi.

"No! Little girl–stop!" He bade her, clasping her shoulder in a steely grip and spinning her around to face him.

Her face blanched in astonishment at the sight of him. She did a low curtsy, holding onto the edges of her dress as she dipped near the ground.

"My Lord Dracula!" She gasped.

Bela smiled and chuckled. Rubbing the fabric of his cape with one of his thumbs absently, an expression of false modesty upon his face. "Well, no, actually it is I, Bela Lugosi! But I do play Dracula in films. Indeed, it was I who first originated the role upon the silver screen, forever immortalizing the definitive interpretation and setting the bar to a height that few can hope to ever surpass!"

"Oh. So, just another ghost then." She said dismissively as she whirled around hungrily to face her dinner–me–once more.

"Not just 'another ghost'!" Bela bristled, "but a ghost that knows where all the tastiest morsels in town are."

This caught her attention. Her eyes widened and she tilted her head to face him again.

"Really?"

"Yes, really! Trust me, Bobb here is a good guy, he's my buddy, but you wouldn't like the way he tastes. I know where all the best necks in town are. Delectable necks! Glorious necks! Necks like you wouldn't believe! Leave this one be."

Then he stared right at her with that flinty gaze of his and waved one hand in her direction, a hand that was splayed out and contorted like the talon of some great, nameless bird of prey. Or perhaps a carrion bird?

"Never trouble this one again." He said as if trying to mesmerize her.

"Well, okay, I guess. So you really do know the best spots to eat around here?"

"Hey! Would the king of the Vampires lie to you?"

"But you said that you're not really Dracula, that you just played Dracula in some old movies..."

"Fine! If you're going to keep on splitting hairs like that, then I won't share my dining tips with you! I'm the next best thing to the real Dracula, I tell you! In fact, one might say that I'm more authentically Dracula than the real Dracula is! Have you ever met him? Ugh! Such a disappointment! No style! No grace! And the table manners of a wild goat! Impale this! Impale that! He's really quite a bore."

"No, no, no! Show me! I want to know where all the best food is!" She pleaded.

He smiled down at her almost paternalistically. "Stick with me, my child. I have such sights to show you." He took her hand and together they walked through my wall and disappeared back into whatever twilight world they had come from.

I fought for a breath like a diver breaking the surface of the ocean, a cold sweat upon my brow. Was it all just a dream? It felt so real! Of course it was all just a dream. It had to be right?

But to this day, whenever I see a picture of Bela Lugosi, or see him on a screen, I give silent praise to him for that night. That strange night so many years ago now, when he saved me from the ignominious destiny of being an unremarkable meal. I don't know how or why he seems to have such a fondness for me, or how I ever earned his esteem. Perhaps we were friends in some now forgotten past life? Fellow dope fiends riding the snake together? However it may have happened, Bela Lugosi is my Guardian Angel, my Guardian Angel clad in black white and red.

Wherever you are right now Bela, thank you.

CASUALTY VAMPIRES

*W*hat strange times to be alive, Allison thought ruefully as she watched the golden disk of the sun slide ever further down the line of the horizon from the top of the old Ferris wheel. She was reflecting on the various recent revelations about the nature of what was real and what wasn't which had been rocking her world.

Especially since I'm technically not alive anymore.

The thought still startled her. Yet as unbelievable as it was, the truth of it was inescapable. All she had to do to confirm it was put her fingers on her carotid artery and feel for a pulse that would never be there again. Or think about how she had made it to the top of the rusted hulk of a Ferris wheel where she now sat. She'd leapt up here in a single bound, like Superman. Such abilities were one of the few perks of being a walking corpse, she supposed.

Yet as thrilling as such powers were, ultimately it was poor compensation for what she'd traded away in exchange for them.

No, not traded. Been forced to give up, she corrected herself.

So many of the events that had led her here were still such a blur. Fragmented snapshots of various moments in time:

dark, winding country roads slick with torrential rain, her mother's shrill screams as the car suddenly flipped upside down, her body being shot through with pain as she was flung from the wreck. Awakening to see two pale, almost angelically good looking faces peering down at her, a man with finely chiseled features and sandy blonde hair, the woman with long ebony locks framing a classically beautiful face.

"This one is still alive, but not for much longer. Not unless we act quickly." One of them said. In her daze, the words sounded like a tape that had been slowed down, so distorted that she couldn't tell which one had spoken.

Next came the bite, a sensation which was barely perceptible since she was already in shock, then the feeling of being drained, the icy chill that gripped her body as her lifeblood ebbed away. Then came the strange overwhelming compulsion, the animalistic thirst for blood that she now always felt on some level or another. Later on, she would discover that on that first occasion, it had been implanted into her mind in order to get her to drink from the gaping wound right above the woman's now bared chest. She had drunk deeply and greedily that night. As she did so, some semblance of her lost warmth returned to her frigid body. In fact, she felt like she had a fever, like her whole body was now aflame. If she'd only known what terrible manner of phoenix would arise from those flames, she would've tried harder to resist the urge to drink that had been put in her head.

She remembered waking up in an unfamiliar room after what felt like an eternity of dreamless sleep. The man and the woman coming to her with their strange explanations, their weak rationalizations for what they'd done to her. It had all been too much to process. She could scarcely deal with the reality that her whole family was dead, her father, her mother and even her annoying little brother.

"You'd be gone forever too, if we hadn't done what we'd done." He told her, like she should bow down and be grateful or something! The arrogance of the man astounded her! How could she be grateful? Grateful for becoming a monster?

And to think, there had been a time when she used to believe that maybe it would be cool to be, to be...(she could barely force herself to even think the word) to be a vampire. This had, of course, been back before she had ever dared to really imagine that such legends might have any kind of a basis in truth. When she had believed them to just be the stuff of late night horror features and cheesy novels. The reality of it wasn't so bad in some ways. She'd learned that it was perfectly safe for her to walk around in broad daylight–the idea that sunlight could kill a vampire was an invention of the people who made that old silent film Nosferatu.

Hence, she was able to safely try to enjoy this sunset. She didn't even have to kill people for the blood she now needed to sustain herself, at least so long as she remained on the farm where she'd been taken to. The Sherwoods, the couple that had "saved" her, had a herd of cattle that they took blood from with syringes, stored and reheated. It was all very humane. Very sustainable.

If the reality of it wasn't so bad, it wasn't so great either though. Immorality didn't seem very appealing when it meant that you were permanently stuck at the age of fourteen. Maybe if she'd been a full grown adult in her twenties or thirties like the other two, it wouldn't be so terrible. But to be stuck in the body of a child forever limited her options in countless ways. It just wasn't fair!

She'd wished that they'd left her to die in the road on that night, then she'd be with her family, her real family, not stuck in this endless half-life.

"We always wanted a child of our own, a daughter. But of course, dead things can't give birth to new life. This is the closest we can come to doing that." The woman had said, revealing their true motivations for "rescuing" her that night. It hadn't been done out of altruism, but out of a twisted desire for a child. But Allison already had parents, parents that she still loved, parents that she missed with all her heart, parents that she longed to be with. She didn't want new ones, nobody could ever replace her real Mom and Dad, least of all not Mr. and Mrs. Dracula!

She'd tried to starve herself, to refuse the reheated dishes of blood that were prepared for her and brought up to her room by the human servants that tended to them.

It had been impossible.

Her need for blood was as bad as any drug addiction that she'd ever heard about. Even worse, probably. She'd had lurid fantasies about attacking those servants and sucking them dry when they entered her room with a bowl of blood on a tray. She could hear the blood rushing through their veins, she could smell it! In the end, the only way she'd been able to avoid becoming a murderer herself was to accept the "food" they offered her, the only kind of food that her magically reanimated body could process any longer. The fact that she couldn't really enjoy any of her favorite things to eat any longer, ever again was just one more major bummer about her predicament to add to the list.

So now here she was. Sitting on top of the Ferris wheel in an abandoned theme park on the edge of town contemplating her next move. She was running away. She didn't know where she'd go. Maybe she'd live in the forest and prey on the animals that lived there? That sucked too. She loved animals and she didn't know the first thing about trying to survive in the wilderness, but she also knew that she didn't want to hurt anyone else. Yet, she also knew that she couldn't keep on living in that creepy old mansion playing family with those blood sucking freaks.

She had come here once before, back when this place was still open. She'd been barely more than a toddler then, but she still remembered the sweet smell of cotton candy in the air, the tinny, cheerful music wafting from the speakers, the lights and the laughter. Those were good times. Good times when she had been truly alive. Truly alive with her real family.

She was snapped out of her reverie by a sharp presence in the back of her mind. "Shit!" She hissed as she twisted her head back just in time to see the woman, Elizabeth, land beside her with a sudden, metallic *clang* on the superstructure of the Ferris wheel.

"How did you find me?" She said, her voice sounding more resigned than angry. She

hated herself for the surrender in it.

Elizabeth laughed, but not in a cruel or mocking fashion. "You're my Childling, Allison. My blood courses through yours, in many ways we are one now. Forever linked. I'll always be able to find you, if I really put my mind to it."

"I suppose you're here to force me to come back, like you forced me to drink your blood that night?" Allison asked bitterly. "When do I get a choice? When do I get a chance to decide how I'm going to spend the rest of my eternity?"

"You're wrong. I won't force you to come back with me. Maybe it was wrong of us to force you into this life, maybe it was selfish." She paused, her voice weighed down with emotion. It hadn't been easy for her to admit that last part. "But it is what it is now. If you leave, it's only a matter of time before the Hunger makes you do something you'll regret, before it turns you into something that you're not, something that you never wanted to be."

"I'm already something that I never wanted to be!" Allison shouted at her (God! How it felt good to let it out like that!)

"You know what I mean! As bad as things might seem to you now, they can be worse, believe me, they can be much worse. I've been down that road already, so has William. We're

still haunted by the faces of all the people we killed. Even all these centuries later, we still see their terrified faces whenever we close our eyes. I would spare you that pain, if I could. I know we can't ever replace your birth family, but that doesn't mean that we can't try to make the best out of an ugly situation. Please, come back with me. If we can't be family, at least let's try to be friends. Besides, the cows will miss you, and I know you'll miss them." Elizabeth pleaded.

Allison sighed. A part of her wanted to deck the older vampire right in her lovely, self-righteous face so hard that she'd knock her right off of the Ferris wheel. But something about the sheer sincerity in her tone and in her eyes caused her to stay her hand. And dammit, she was right about the cows. They were real cuties, and the one thing Allison would miss about this whole fucked up situation was helping to care for them. How did she know her so well in such a short amount of time? How often and how deeply was she able to get into her head? It just wasn't fair!

Allison smiled, in spite of herself. The sun had already slipped beneath the distant hills and the first twinkling lights of twilight were starting to sparkle in the sky all around them.

"Alright. I guess I'll try hanging around a little longer, at least until I can think of something better to do."

Elizabeth smiled back and held out a hand, her long, delicate fingers flattened out invitingly.

Allison stared at the offered hand for a moment, perhaps pondering all that it represented, then she grasped it fiercely and together the two immortals leapt out into the darkening night....

ALLISON

Form frozen in time

In her books a mind takes flight

Living other lives

THE LOST LENORE

Martin Lane stared at the thing outside of his window, transfixed. He couldn't quite tell if it was a wolf or a bear. Surely it was too big to be a wolf? Besides, there were no wolves left in this state, hadn't been for quite a while (no matter what nonsense the news said about that poor girl who'd been found dead in Shadowbrook). Yet, the shape was all wrong, definitely more wolfish. The gray, hairy thing in fact looked very much like what he'd imagined a dire wolf to look like from those fantasy novels he sometimes read.

Of course, there was another possibility, but it was one that was too terrible to contemplate. No, surely, it couldn't be one of *them.*

Whatever it was, he couldn't stand here all day gaping at it from his kitchen. He couldn't

let it get near his cattle. They were his livelihood (in more ways than one). His property was surrounded by a barbed wire fence, but it wasn't very hard for him to imagine this thing being able to leap over it.

Martin shook himself out of his stupor, ran to the back door and reached for the old shotgun that was leaning up against the nearby wall. Why did he suddenly find himself wishing that the shot it was loaded with was made of silver?

It wasn't one of them, it couldn't be! There had been no sign of them in all his travels. No evidence that they'd ever existed outside of William and Elizabeth's stories. He'd half convinced himself that they were just a product of his old friends' imaginations.

He tried to focus on the here and now, on keeping the thing away from his small herd which was peacefully grazing nearby. As he swung open the door, he stepped out onto the edge of his back porch and aimed his rifle into the air, letting off a warning shot. His cattle, which he could now see over on the next hill, immediately scattered at the sound of the sharp report. If he'd expected the beast on the other side of the fence to follow suit, he would be sorely disappointed.

It still stood there, looking back at him.

Yes, definitely not normal animal behavior, Martin thought soberly.

Yet in that moment, Martin felt something like a mental connection between himself and the creature had briefly formed, and within that connection, there was no sense of malice. If anything, he felt a feeling of weariness, of resignation, perhaps twinged with a touch of disappointment. Martin and the thing remained like that, looking into each other's eyes for a few more seconds before the beast suddenly turned its back on him and disappeared into the underbrush from which it had first emerged like it had all been nothing but a bad dream.

Martin found himself wishing that's what it was, just a bad dream. He wanted desperately to believe that's all that it was. He had to walk over to the edge of his property and look over the fence at the ground where the thing had been standing, to see for himself the tracks it had left behind in the soft earth that was still moist from last light's downpour, before he'd allow himself to believe in the reality of it.

There was no doubt about it. That thing had been exactly what he'd feared it was—a werewolf. How else could it have reached out to touch his mind like that? Elizabeth and William had said that they could do that with people like them. The werewolves could sense the presence of vampires and form empathetic connections with them. In fact, this was why they had been created in the first place, to act as guard dogs, enforcers for the Master that he used to keep his flock in line. William and Elizabeth had hoped that the werewolves had all been destroyed back in England, along with the rest of the vampires, when they had escaped from the Master centuries earlier.

They'd been wrong about the vampires, though. Was it such a surprise that they were also wrong about the werewolves? Martin had encountered a few fellow vampires during his travels, aside from Lenore, of course. They'd always been strange, tense meetings. The other vampires were as frightened of him and Lenore as they were of them. Both parties were typically unfamiliar with others of their kind and didn't know if they could trust them. These other vampires seemed to know nothing of the Master, or the history of their kind that had been told to him by William and Elizabeth. They had been created and then abandoned by their sires for whatever reason, wandering the earth in confusion. Martin had always been grateful that William and Elizabeth hadn't done that to him, he'd been grateful for the knowledge of what he was that they'd shared with him.

Yet at this moment, that knowledge brought him little comfort. If a werewolf was near his property, it was no coincidence. Werewolves were used by the Master to hunt down and kill disobedient vampires. True, he'd felt no ill intent from this particular one when their minds had temporarily collided, but then there was that story about the girl in Shadowbrook. Something had broken into her room and torn her apart, something that the authorities were convinced had been a wolf. Martin had scoffed at the idea when the story broke. Not only because of the fact that there were no wolves left in these parts, but because he knew how wolves behaved from back in the days when there had been plenty of them around. He knew that they didn't usually come crashing through the bedroom windows in suburban neighborhoods.

Yet it perfectly fits the M.O. of a werewolf. The creature he'd just seen had to be the culprit. He knew that just as he had learned to control his lust for blood by feeding off of the few heads of cattle he kept on his modest farm, werewolves could similarly sustain themselves by hunting other animals, just like regular wolves did. Just as Martin had when he had been traveling. There was no need for them to attack humans. They had more control over themselves in their bestial form than popular fiction would have you believe. In fact, from what he'd been told by Elizabeth and William, the Master often forbade them from attacking humans precisely because of the unwanted attention it tended to attract. So the fact that this particular werewolf had attacked that girl was a deliberate and viscous choice it had made. The werewolf had to be some kind of a psychopath that enjoyed killing.

If he bore no particular ill will towards Martin, perhaps it was because it was merely doing its job, using its power to track vampires so that the others could come later on to deal with him and do the actual killing. William and Elizabeth had mentioned this too. Sometimes wayward vampires would be culled by other vampires once they'd been located and sometimes the Master himself would do it. But why show itself like it had? It was probably an accident that it had been spotted, but why linger once he'd been seen? Why reach out to touch Martin's mind?

Martin didn't know the answers to these questions, but he wondered if it was really such a bad thing that they'd found him? Was it so bad that his long life might really be coming to its end? What an odd thought this was for him to be entertaining! He, who had once been so fearful of death, now being so blasé about it finally coming to claim him! His overwhelming fixation with his own mortality had begun when an outbreak of cholera had claimed most of his friends and family in his hamlet back in England.

The plague had destroyed his faith in God as surely as it had the lives of those closest to him. How could a benevolent creator allow such horrific things to happen? No, he had become sure at that point that life was just inherently cruel, random and uncertain. There was no Lord in Heaven watching out for you. No matter how hard you prayed, death would come for you someday–or worse, the ones you loved first. He was just as certain that there was no life beyond this one either. No great reward awaiting us beyond. An icy fear gripped his heart whenever he had allowed himself to contemplate the endless nothingness that lay in store for him. The incomprehensibleness of nonexistence vexed him constantly; it terrified him.

Chance had singled him out for survival, and he had resolved to do what he could to make the most of what life he had left to him. Having inherited some money from relatives of his that had been claimed by the disease, he left behind the plague blighted land of his birth. He couldn't stand to be there any longer, it now held too many painful memories. Instead, he'd booked passage on a ship and set sail for the promise of opportunity in the New World.

It was on this transatlantic voyage that he had first met William and Elizabeth and had leapt at the opportunity they represented. The opportunity to cheat the Reaper as surely as he had been cheated of the joy of ever seeing his lost relatives and friends again! A normal man would've recoiled in horror at the sight of the two of them when he chanced upon them: their hungry mouths streaked with the blood of the bilge rats they'd taken to feeding on during the long voyage, the miserable little creatures still squealing and squirming in their frigid hands. But Martin Lane was no ordinary man anymore. Death had hardened him. In an instant he knew what they really were. He hadn't imagined that such things were real, and yet here they were, right in front of him!

He'd offered himself up right then and there. They could feed on him for the rest of their journey, surely that would be preferable to scrounging for rats in the deepest bowels of the vessel? But they must not drink too deeply, for in exchange for his life's blood they would have to agree to make him like they were when they arrived in America. To their credit, they'd tried to talk him out of it. Told him that he didn't understand what he was asking them for, didn't understand how difficult it was to resist the urge to rip into the throats of every human they came across. They tried to speak to him of the burden of immortality, of how he would never change and grow old while those closest to him did. He'd just laughed at them. "I have no one left to me who is close! If we only have this one life to us, I intend to live it to the fullest—to the longest! I shall avoid oblivion for as long as I possibly can!" He'd argued. Besides, if they didn't give him what he wanted, he'd threatened to report them to the rest of the crew. They could kill him to prevent such a thing, of course, but they were obviously trying to avoid killing people anymore, so he'd wagered that they wouldn't. His ability to read them had been spot on. In the end, he'd worn them down with his mixture of arguments and threats. He got what he'd wanted.

The unusual intimacy of allowing them to feed off of him had also led to them becoming close in other ways. By the time the weeks-long ocean voyage had ended, they had become the best of friends. They remained together once they'd disembarked for shore. Martin had helped them select the land to purchase that they would transform into their farm, had lent his hands to the building of the handsome mansion that was to become their home. All of this was accomplished with the treasure they'd stolen from the Master when they'd made their escape from him.

It had been one of the happiest periods of Martin's unnaturally long life, but all good things must eventually come to an end, and this was no exception. As the years spent together turned into decades, Martin grew weary of his life on the dairy farm. He had lost sight of his original goal in seeking immortality. He had all of eternity to explore the world, to see every inch of it, to seek out every nook and cranny, yet he had failed to do so! He couldn't possibly live life to the fullest stuck in this remote corner of Connecticut. And so it was that he said his goodbyes to the two friends who had become his family and set out on the great adventure of his life.

All the wonderful places he would travel to! First mostly in the Americans, then later, once airplanes had made international travel faster, all over the world.

It had been an exciting, yet lonely existence at first. Lonely, that is, until he met his Lenore. The thought of when he first saw her sitting alone and looking perfectly lovely at that little bar in San Francisco still made him smile, even now after all these years. It had taken all of his courage to walk up to her and strike up a conversation. In her he'd found a kindred spirit, someone who was always as up for any new adventure as he had been. He'd shared everything with her, even the secret of what he truly was. When she found out, she begged him to make her like he was, just as he had when he first happened upon Elizabeth and William. It was at that moment that he knew she was the one he'd been waiting his whole life for.

The first few decades they'd spent together had been magical, there wasn't any other way to describe it. She had been the good and faithful companion that he'd never known he'd needed. He'd never loved anyone else so deeply, so completely. But in retrospect, he'd come to realize that he'd done an inadequate job of preparing her for what life as a vampire would be like, he'd failed to explain the disadvantages of immortality, because for him there were no real disadvantages. It was different for her though, she wasn't quite as...untethered to the rest of the world as he was. She still had family and friends that she was attached to.

They'd found clever ways to fake aging when they dropped in to visit them, using wigs and makeup. But in time, there came a point where the charade became unsustainable, when it started to look too ridiculous. They'd been forced to cut off communications with them then, in order to maintain their secrets.

This had broken her heart and she never truly recovered from it. She fell into a deep depression that even their globetrotting escapades couldn't cure. Martin had never felt so helpless as he watched her doldrums come to consume her. He'd known she'd been unhappy, but he'd never truly understood exactly how deep the river of her melancholy ran. He hadn't understood until he came home to find that she'd taken her own life–no easy feat for one of their kind.

Contrary to popular belief, sunlight didn't kill them. The stake through the heart, while it was certainly unpleasant, was not particularly fatal. Its true purpose was to pin them in place long enough to decapitate them–the only thing that truly killed them. Even then, supposedly, there were ways to reanimate them unless the neck was stuffed with garlic and the body set ablaze, although such a resurrection required the services of a wizard or witch to effect. Martin didn't know where to find a magic user, and even if he had, he wouldn't have dared to disrespect her wishes like that. So she was gone now, and she would remain so, forever. Martin could still scarcely imagine how deeply troubled she must've been to have the determination to cut off her own head. Such sorrow was unimaginable to him. Or at least it had been, until he'd lost her.

He'd returned to "home" in Connecticut after Lenore had passed and tried to settle down. He'd copied William and Elizabeth's method of keeping cattle to satiate his thirst for blood. Although, every so often, when he needed a bit of variety and excitement, he would still hunt in the forest for his food as he had when he'd been traveling.

He didn't live very far from Elizabeth and William's old place now, which they'd named "Sherwood Farm", yet he'd never come by to visit. Ever since Lenore had committed suicide, he'd feared what he might find at the farm. He worried that perhaps the weight of the centuries had caught up to his old friends as well, bringing them to also kill themselves. Or perhaps the

Hunger had been too powerful (cow's blood really was a poor substitute for human blood) and they'd reverted to their old ways?) He himself had even given into his darker impulses on a few rare occasions, although he typically tried to reserve such things for those whom he felt deserved some kind of punishment. William and Elizabeth had always been more idealistic than he was. He couldn't stand to see them reduced to becoming the very thing they'd despised. No, it was better to remember them as they were than to see what time might've transformed them into. His heart couldn't take another loss like that, not after what he'd suffered when Lenore had left him.

It was undeniably true that he had been finding little joy in life since he'd lost his beloved Lenore. Maybe his days of trying to outrun the Reaper *should* come to an end? He had also encountered some Ghosts during his many journeys around the earth, and so he no longer believed that death was truly the end. There was obviously something more, although he knew not what. The idea of being a ghost wasn't very appealing to him, either. Yet, if every soul didn't become a specter bound to this world as some people believed, maybe he could someday reunite with Lenore, and all the others he'd lost?

Yes, perhaps when the Reaper next came for him, he'd just let him take him this time.

He'd had a good life. He'd been many things over the years: a thief, an explorer, gambler, a lover–hell, sometimes even a hero in spite of himself. Death might be the only new adventure left to him. He could run. He had a small fortune hidden away which he had acquired over the centuries through a mixture of guile, luck and outright thievery, but perhaps it was better to just let fate take its course? Perhaps in death he'd finally find the peace that had eluded him on this farm?

He'd made up his mind. When they came for him. He'd stand and face them.

He wouldn't have long to wait. When he returned to his house that night after finishing up his chores, they were waiting for him inside. He could sense them as he approached the house, but he made no attempt to flee. Even if he'd wanted to, he probably couldn't. The woods surrounding his property were full of them. He could feel them watching him from the tree line as he'd gone about his work for that final hour before heading back inside.

There were two of them this time. One was a werewolf, although it looked nothing like the creature he'd seen in the field earlier that day. This werewolf was in a bipedal form, which bore something of a resemblance to Lon Chaney Jr.'s portrayal of the Wolfman. Except this particular Wolfman had a gait that was stopped with age. He had unruly, long gray fur, and mournful looking eyes that flashed with intelligence. He was dressed rather shabbily in a drab, badly stretched out pair of sweatpants with a mismatched sweatshirt. He wore some kind of a cloak and a leather messenger bag bulging with books dangled off of one shoulder. Martin wasn't particularly surprised by this werewolf. He'd been told that they could shift freely between different forms on the spectrum between man and wolf.

The second intruder was the opposite of his companion. He was a tall, muscular man with long, lustrous black hair and a clean shaven, square jawed face. He was dressed in somewhat antiquated clothes, wearing a loose fitting white shirt with a large, frilly collar and puffy sleeves which would've been in fashion back in Martin's native era. He looked like a refugee from a renaissance fair, or maybe the cover of a romance novel about pirates. Obviously, this one was a vampire, and one who was intent upon living up to all the latest cliches about their kind. The guy had probably seen Interview with the Vampire too many times. The thought made Martin grin, despite the gravity of the situation. Something about them was oddly familiar, like he should know who they were already.

They had both been standing in the center of his living room, and as Martin entered the room they swung around to face him simultaneously.

"Please, don't be alarmed. We aren't here to hurt you." The vampire promised in a voice that was deep and mellifluous, the voice of a radio announcer or a master thespian. It only added to his over the top air of savoir faire. Martin actually had to stop himself from giggling. Or perhaps that was just his nervousness? Maybe he didn't have anything to fear from these two after all? They did seem faintly ridiculous.

"I see. And whom do I have the pleasure of addressing?" Martin asked, more amusement in his tone than fear.

"I am known as Blake, and this is my lieutenant, Prospero." The man informed him.

"Blake? I'm confused. Is that your last name or your first name?"

"Why does it matter? It's simply "Blake", that's all you need to understand!" The man, Blake, said, sounding somewhat annoyed and defensive. Martin must've inadvertently struck a sore spot.

"Don't mind him, Laddie," The werewolf rumbled out in an unmistakable Scottish accent. "He doesn't remember anymore, he's a bit sensitive about it."

Martin had heard of this too. Apparently, very old vampires began to lose the memories of their earlier years after a few centuries. Many of them couldn't even remember ever being human.

"You're one to talk! As if "Prospero" is actually your real name! Admit it! Your memory is every bit as bad as mine!" Blake shot back.

Martin's eyes widened in alarm. He suddenly recalled who these two were! Of course! Blake and Prospero! He knew them both from William and Elizabeth's tales of the old days, when they'd all been servants of the Master. Blake was indeed an old vampire, he was one of the Undying Ones, the Master's elite inner circle! In fact, he was none other than his second in command! It had been Blake who had stolen away Elizabeth shortly after she and William had been married. Snatched her up when she went outside to fetch a pail of water from the well. He had made her into a vampire, using his power to seduce her into all manner of unspeakable debauchery. In time, he'd grown tired of her and moved on to fresh conquests.

When the Master wanted to expand his ranks, she'd been allowed to go back to William, who was still beside himself with grief over her disappearance and turned him into a vampire too. Desperate to be reunited with his beloved no matter what the costs, William had accepted.

They'd both served under Blake's terrible command, committing atrocity after atrocity at his direction until they became sick of the endless killing. They'd betrayed the whole group when the first decent opportunity presented itself, making good with their escape across the sea.

If this truly was Blake, then he was extremely dangerous, despite his somewhat comical manner. Prospero too, although Martin recalled that his friends had spoken kindlier of the werewolf. Apparently, he'd served as a moderating influence upon Blake, reigning in his more outlandish impulses, if not his fashion sense.

"I'll admit nothing! My mind is as sharp as it ever was, as sharp as a tack, in fact! It's a good deal sharper than yours, I'll wager!" Prospero growled back (literally).

Blake bellowed in laughter. "I wouldn't make that bet, old man, you're sure to lose! Alright then, if your mind is so sharp, tell me what was your mother's name?"

"Why Evangeline, of course!" Prospero replied, not missing a beat.

"Evangeline?" Blake laughed even harder. "No, no, no my friend! You're quite confused! The only Evangeline we've ever met was that delightful young lady in Budapest back in '67! You know, the one with the enormous bosoms?" He held out his hands in front of his chest, miming and no doubt exaggerating the dimensions of the aforementioned bosoms. "Although, as I recall, she did have you crying out for your mother several times!" He added with a salacious wink.

Jesus! These two bicker like an old married couple! Martin thought. His patience was beginning to wear thin, wishing that they'd just get on with it and kill him already if that was their plan. Anything was better than listening to this idiotic double act.

"Gentlemen!" He barked at them (although not as literally as Prospero would've)

"Please! If I may! Can we focus on the matter at hand? I'd like to know what you are doing in my home, and why you have seen fit to surround my property with others like us if, as you claim, you truly mean no threat to me."

"Yes, of course. I apologize. Sensed them did you? See, he's stronger than you thought. The blood isn't all that diluted in this one!" Blake said.

Prospero grumbled something incoherent in response.

"Those soldiers are there to protect you, not to harm you." Blake continued.

"Protect me? From what exactly? From the werewolf I saw this morning? The same one that killed that poor girl in Shadowbrook?"

"No, the werewolf you saw this morning was me! And that incident in Shadowbrook was the work of Kilroy!" Prospero protested.

"Kilroy?" Martin repeated with a shudder. He knew that name too, according to William and Elizabeth, it was the name of the Master's favorite, the most brutal of all the werewolves.

"Yes. Do you know of him?" Blake inquired, catching onto the recognition in Martin's reaction.

"Only by reputation." Martin confessed.

"If we could find you, then he will too. He's likely on his way here right now. Hence the protection." Prospero chimed in.

"What would he want with me?"

"Why, to kill you of course! You see, there's a war going on. And the other side is desperate to maintain their numerical advantage over us. They're actively seeking out any unaligned vampires or werewolves and killing them before they can join our cause." Blake informed him.

"Cause? What would that be?"

"I intend to end, for all time, the curse of vampirism. It is our belief that if we destroy the beast that is the source of the curse, whose blood runs through all of our veins, that we shall all be returned to humans." Blake announced with a grandiose flourish.

This boast sent Martin's mind reeling. The beast he mentioned was a kind of demon that the Undying Ones called "the Dark Mother". It had been conjured ages ago by the Master, who became the first vampire by drinking the blood of the immortal creature. Apparently, they still kept the demon prisoner, worshiping it in some kind of mysterious ceremonies.

"Is such a thing possible? What makes you believe that would work?" Martin demanded.

"I found the secret, buried in Mortus Locke's own spell books!" Prospero said with a touch of pride, as he patted the messenger bag hanging from his side. Mortus Locke being the true name of the Master, Martin was astounded that Prospero spoke it so freely. William and Elizabeth had feared that he could hear you if you ever said it aloud.

"Once we have grown our forces sufficiently, we will attack and destroy the Dark Mother." Blake declared. "But it's difficult to locate new recruits, especially with Locke's forces constantly seeking to destroy them before we can get to them."

There were several things about all of this which made no sense to Martin.

"Excuse me, but why don't you simply create more vampires and werewolves instead of searching for ones that already exist?"

Blake and Prospero exchanged horrified glances. "That would be…unethical. You see, my followers no longer drink blood."

Martin was flabbergasted. "They don't drink blood? Then how do they survive?"

"I discovered that it's not necessary. It's merely a powerful compulsion. The immortal blood of the Dark Mother that's inside us all is what actually sustains us." Blake confided.

"Aye, it's all in the spell books." Prospero confirmed.

"This is all a bit much to take in." Martin breathed. Not necessarily to drink blood to survive? It was unthinkable! He stretched out his mind to briefly touch theirs and he could feel their sincerity.

"Yes, quite understandable." Blake agreed.

"I also find it quite difficult to believe in this change of heart of yours. Wanting to end the curse? Abstaining from drinking any blood? You have a reputation too, and these sentiments are quite at odds with it!"

"I have come to see…the error of my ways. It's been a long journey to come to that realization, and an even longer story. I'm afraid there's simply no time to tell it right now. All you need to understand is that I wish to make amends and finally put an end to all the killing. I can tell that such things matter to you as well, otherwise you wouldn't be keeping livestock for their blood." Blake said in a halting voice that Martin guessed was as close as the man could ever get to a display of humility.

"I suppose you'd like me to join your little crusade? Become an obedient little soldier for your worthy cause? Is that what brings you here?" Martin scoffed. These two clowns barely seemed capable of organizing a birthday party, let alone leading an army of supernatural creatures. Perhaps Blake had been formidable once, but the centuries had clearly softened him into a parody of his former self.

"Yes, in so many words. My friend, you'll find that unfortunately you don't have many alternatives. It's either join us or allow them to destroy you. Mortus Locke has been rather more paranoid than usual since I rebelled against him. He's not interested in recruiting anyone–he can barely bring himself to trust the ones who are already with him. He'll just destroy you to make sure you'll never come to stand against him." Blake pleaded.

"And you must decide quickly. Kilroy is on his way. We must always stay ahead of him; we can't afford to tarry here for days on end while you mull it over." Prospero added.

"You know, I thought that you were the Master, or his agents, when I entered this house just now. I was already prepared to die. It's been a long, good life, but I'm tired now–I'm ready. I no longer fear death as I once did." Martin was surprised to hear himself admitting such a personal thing to two relative strangers.

"Are ya daft, man? You'll just let them come and rip you to shreds? That's no proper way to die! If yer gonna die, go down swinging! Fighting for a decent cause! Go down with some dignity! Ya canna just give up!" An outraged Prospero shouted. His accent became more pronounced, as it often did when he became overly emotional.

Blake held up a hand and Prospero closed his mouth, looking down in embarrassment at his outburst. Blake spoke to Martin in an unusually tender way for the otherwise boisterous and ebullient man.

"Friend, please consider what we are offering. This is not just an opportunity to do something worthwhile, but a chance to regain our lost humanity. To know what it's like to grow old, to have children. All the things which we, as vampires, have been denied these many years. Think about that."

Martin sank into a nearby armchair as he considered their words. Perhaps death was not the only adventure left to him after all? It had been so long since he'd lived as a mortal that he barely recalled what it was like. To experience a more normal kind of life was about the only kind of thing that he hadn't already done. He still wasn't sure if having children was something he ever wanted to do, but sometimes he thought that it would be interesting to see what it would be like to age like everyone else did. To not have to hide who he really was and form stronger bonds with the people around him.

And if they failed–and they likely would with these two fools running things–then he would still get his wish and end up dead anyway. He hated to admit it, but the werewolf was right. It was better to go out fighting than to just meekly accept the inevitable. It suited his adventurous spirit far more to do so. At any rate, it would be interesting to see what happened next. Whatever did happen was bound to be more exciting than just hanging around on this farm. Who was he trying to fool? He'd really never been cut out to be a farmer, he didn't know why he'd ever bothered to try.

His eyes wandered up to a photo of himself and Lenore in front of the Great Pyramid which sat upon his mantlepiece. Such happy times! Didn't he owe this to her? Surely, there must be other vampires out there like her, tired of the lies and longing for a normal life. Perhaps they were on the verge of suicide too? He'd been unable to save her, but maybe he could save the next Lenore by helping to break the curse?

"Alright. I'll do it." He said.

"Excellent! You see, Prospero? I knew the fellow would come to his senses!" Boasted Blake.

Prospero responded with a low growl, and by waiving one hairy hand dismissively. "My friend, I promise you won't regret it!"

Blake beamed at him, offering his hand.

Martin clasped the man's large, cool, beefy hand. He didn't know what this new adventure would bring, but he knew that whatever it brought, he would face it bravely, for Lenore and perhaps most importantly, for himself.

Yes, he decided with a smile, he did have time for one last adventure after all....

MORTUS LOCKE

I do what I do
constantly dominating
I know nothing else

KILLROY

I am the hunter
On your knees, prey to me now
Your flesh is my flesh

Robert Enrico Sohl is the collective consciousness of billions of units of microscopic organic matter. He was born and raised in southern New Jersey but has resided in Virginia for the last few decades. He is a husband and the father to two rather peculiar offspring. He is the author and illustrator of the *Dead End World* series of novels chronicling the unusual adventures of Matt Spike, P.I., and his friends. In addition to those tales, he also enjoys writing horror and fantasy short stories.

OTHER BOOKS IN THE DEAD END WORLD SAGA:

The Shadow of Death

Tales from a Dead End World

Beyond the Veil of Death

Tales from a Dead End World Volume 2

Matt Spike and the Vampire's Curse

Jersey Devils

Coming in 2024:

Night of The Mothman

Matt Spike Against the Amazon Saucer Women from Venus

Tales From A Dead End World Volume 3

Milton Keynes UK
Ingram Content Group UK Ltd.
UKHW020843220224
438295UK00013B/410

9 781959 860334